Sunny

Rishelle.

Nick

ELMO

LIZ

D1446699

EMILY RODDA'S RAVEN HILL MYSTERIES

#1: THE GHOST OF RAVEN HILL

Look for Emily Rodda's next Raven Hill Mystery:

Case #2: The Sorcerer's Apprentice

EMILY RODDA'S
RAVEN HILL MYSTERIES

#1: THE GHOST OF RAVEN HILL

Emily Rodda

APPLE · SERIES

SCHOLASTIC INC.

New York Toronto London Auckland Sydney
Mexico City New Delhi Hong Kong Buenos Aires

No part of this publication may be reproduced, stored in a retrieval system, or transmitted in any form or by any means, electronic, mechanical, photocopying, recording, or otherwise, without written permission of the publisher. For information regarding permission, write to Permissions Department, Scholastic Australia, P.O. Box 579, Lindfield, New South Wales, Australia 2070.

ISBN 0-439-79770-5

Series concept copyright © 1994 by Emily Rodda
Text copyright © 1994 by Scholastic Australia

All rights reserved. Published by Scholastic Inc., 557 Broadway, New York, NY 10012, by arrangement with Scholastic Press, an imprint of Scholastic Australia.

SCHOLASTIC, APPLE PAPERBACKS, and associated logos are trademarks and/or registered trademarks of Scholastic Inc.

12 11 10 9 8 7 6 5 4 3 2 1   5 6 7 8 9 10/0

Printed in the U.S.A.
First Scholastic printing, September 2005

EMILY RODDA'S
RAVEN HILL MYSTERIES

#1: THE GHOST OF RAVEN HILL

Contents

1

The beginning

"I'm starving! And I'm broke," moaned Tom. "Penniless. Cleaned out. Poverty-stricken. Destitute."

"Join the club," said Sunny.

"What's new?" Richelle yawned at the same moment.

Nick didn't say anything. But his scowl said plenty.

"If only we had part-time jobs –" I began. But they all groaned.

"There *aren't* any jobs, Liz. You know that," sighed Sunny.

"Don't be negative, Sunny Chan," Tom scolded, rolling his eyes. "You're forgetting. Queen Lizzie has magical powers. She's going to *make* us some jobs. Aren't you, Your Majesty?"

I opened my mouth to shout at him. And then, suddenly, I had my brilliant idea. The idea that was going to make us all some money. The idea (though I didn't know it then) that was going to put us all up to our necks in trouble!

"Yes," I said calmly. "That's just what I'm going to do. Make us some jobs."

Sunny started knotting herself into a complicated yoga pose. I think she'd given up on me.

Tom leaned his chin on his hand. "Speak, wise one," he begged earnestly.

I tried to ignore him.

"This is what we do," I said. "We *advertise* ourselves. As a group. We call ourselves something that'll attract attention. Like . . . say . . . Help-for-Hire. To make it clear we're here to help out people."

Nick sighed heavily.

"And we say we'll do anything," I said.

Tom raised his eyebrows and opened his mouth.

"Within reason," I added quickly. I could see he was going to say something stupid like: What about lion taming? Or drug smuggling?

"Liz Free's fourteen-day poverty plan!" Tom exclaimed in his best TV ad voice. "Buy now and achieve total destitution in weeks! Plus, you get a set of stainless steel headaches absolutely free!"

Nick, agreeing with Tom for once in his life, looked scornfully down his nose at me. Sunny said nothing. Richelle, of course, just yawned and went on checking her hair for split ends. My dog, Monty, was paying more attention than she was.

We were in the Glen at the time. That's the patch of forest next to the park down at the end of my block. We knew that soon it would be sold and torn apart. We felt bad about that.

In elementary school, our gang had played in the Glen. And now that we were at Raven Hill High, we still went there to talk. It was quiet, except for birds, and cool all year-round. People said it was haunted, but the Glen Ghost had never bothered us. Up till then, anyway. That problem was still to come.

I looked around at the kids sprawled on the ground. Tom, gangly and skinny, sketching as usual; Sunny, small and energetic, now doing leg stretches; clever, dark-eyed computer-whiz Nick, chewing a stick and looking at the sky; beautiful, oblivious Richelle, who had now moved on from her split ends to her fingernails.

"Well?" I demanded.

"So we spend a fortune on an ad and end up with dog walking and babysitting," sneered Nick, spitting out his stick.

I nearly lost my temper. "Well, we have to do something, Nick! Our school break starts at the end of next week. And other things will come in as well."

Nick looked disgusted. I racked my brains for interesting jobs. "You and Sunny and I can type, so there's that," I said. "Or someone having a party might want us to help clean up. Or say a recording company needed a group of kids to be extras in a music video. They could call us."

Richelle raised her eyes and blinked at me. I congratulated myself. The music video idea had been an inspiration.

"We may as well try it," she drawled. Then added, in case anyone thought she was too into it: "Nothing else to do."

She looked at her hands again. But I knew she wasn't really examining her nail polish. She was imagining herself being "discovered" on the set of the music video. "That girl over there," the director would be saying, "the one with the superb mane of hair and the beautiful eyes. Richelle, isn't it? Put her in front."

Typically, as soon as Richelle said okay, everyone else fell into line. It's infuriating, the way that happens. But I catch myself doing it, too. Maybe it's because Richelle is usually so cool and bored that you think well, if she wants to do something, it must be really worth doing.

"Do we advertise in the *Pen* or the *Star*?" asked practical Sunny.

"The *Pen*'s old-fashioned," said Nick.

"The *Star*'s garbage," sneered Tom.

They started arguing about the rival local newspapers. I was pleased. At least now they were fighting about *how* we'd go ahead, not *if*. My worries were over.

Or so I thought. In fact, of course, they were just beginning.

We took ages to work out what to put in the ad, and especially what to call ourselves. Nick suggested a name made up of initials, but when Tom started getting silly and suggesting things like TWIRP (Totally Weird, Inane Rip-off Plus) and BUMS (Brainy, Useful, Muscled Stars), he gave up on the idea.

In the end, we settled on Help-for-Hire after all. But we added Inc. to the end of it. Nick said that would make us sound well organized, like a real business.

I finally wrote the ad on Wednesday, sitting under the apple tree at school with everyone else looking over my shoulder. "HELP-FOR-HIRE INC. Five responsible, mature teenagers . . ." I began.

Tom said that calling us responsible and mature was false advertising and we'd end up in jail. Nick said that while in Tom's case that was so, the rest of us would be okay. Then they started insulting each other and Sunny had to threaten to beat them both up before they'd stop. They knew she could do it, too. So they settled down, and I went on writing.

In the end, the ad read:

HELP-FOR-HIRE INC.
Five responsible, mature teenagers
will tackle any jobs around your house,
garden, shop, or business. Typing
OK, computer OK, children and
pets OK. Raven Hill area only.
Cheap hourly rate. No job too small.
We'll do anything!

I thought it sounded quite good.

We put my own phone number at the bottom. Nick and Tom didn't want the responsibility. Sunny has four older sisters, and her phone's always busy. And no one even thought of giving Richelle's number. She'd be just as likely to write messages on the back of an envelope or something, then wander off and forget all about them.

The ad was going to cost a fortune. Most of the money we scraped together was mine and Nick's. Sunny doesn't get much allowance because her mom already pays for gymnastics, tae kwon do, *and* yoga classes. Tom gets something from his parents every week, but he never saves any. No wonder, the way he eats. The school cafeteria could survive on Tom alone, I swear.

And the day after we had our talk in the Glen, Richelle had

spent every cent she had on a new top. The top was very bare and sexy. I guess she thought it would impress the music video director.

Luckily, I had a little money saved, and Nick did, too. Or maybe he got it from his mother. Nick's an only child, and he has his mom twisted around his little finger.

The others said they'd pay us back when jobs started coming in. I had a little twinge of doubt. What if no jobs came in? Then Tom's joke about Liz Free's poverty plan would be only too true. For me, anyway.

2

It pays to advertise

We'd finally decided to put our ad in the *Pen*. My dad said that since the *Star* started up, the old paper had lost quite a few advertisers. Both papers were free, and they survived only because of paid ads. So I said our money should go to the *Pen*.

Nick said I was just being lame, as usual. But Sunny reminded him that all the old ladies in Raven Hill trusted the *Pen*. They hadn't gotten used to the *Star* yet. And they were the ones who most often needed jobs done around their houses. Nick could see the sense in that, so he backed off.

But when Sunny and I saw the *Pen* building the next afternoon, I started to wonder if we'd made the right choice after all. There was graffiti all over the front, and someone had changed the RAVEN HILL PEN sign at the entrance to read RAVEN HILL PAIN. The only nice thing about the place was the colored-glass window above the door. And it looked out of place, like a jewel in a garbage dump.

As we opened it, the door shrieked as if a parrot was stuck in the hinges. Inside was a small room with grubby light green walls.

Opposite the door hung a framed, spotty sign that read THE PEN
IS MIGHTIER THAN THE SWORD.

The office smelled of old paper and dust. It had a hard-looking
visitors' bench, murky-colored carpet, a huge plastic palm tree in
a pot, and two ancient desks.

Behind one desk sat a cross-looking woman who glared at us
as though she had a lot of personal problems and we'd caused
every one of them. Behind the other desk, a bored-looking girl
with long red fingernails was chewing gum and typing on a computer, very slowly.

The woman narrowed her eyes at us. "Yes?" she snapped.

Sunny nudged me and I held out our precious money. "I – I
called," I stuttered. "About an ad."

The woman clicked her tongue as if the whole thing was a
plot set up just to annoy her. "Bring it here, then," she sighed,
and held out an impatient hand.

I felt like turning around and walking out, but at that moment
a door in the back of the office swung open.

"Miss Moss?" chirped a voice. A small man with a round face
and a tangle of red curly hair popped his head around the door.
He had worry lines on his forehead and his eyes looked tired,
but he smiled shyly at us. The smile somehow reminded me of
someone else.

"Oh, sorry," he said. "I didn't know anyone was here."

The crabby woman sniffed. "A small advertisement, Mr.
Zimmer," she said, as though to warn him that we were no one
important.

"Ah." The man smiled again and ventured into the room.
"May I?" he said, and took the ad from me. He read it, his eyebrows

8

gradually creeping up till they were lost in his curly hair. And then I realized why his smile was so familiar. It was just like Elmo Zimmer's smile.

Elmo was in our year at school. He was a bit of a loner. I remembered someone saying that his mother had died when he was little, and he lived with his dad. Mr. Zimmer must be Elmo's father.

Mr. Zimmer pursed his lips. There was silence for a moment, except for the clicking of the chewing-girl's fingernails on her keyboard. I exchanged glances with Sunny. Was there something wrong with the ad? Or was Mr. Zimmer a bit — odd?

"Fate, Miss Moss!" exclaimed Mr. Zimmer.

My heart skipped a beat. The cranky woman behind the desk looked even angrier than before. "Mr. Zimmer . . ." she began warningly.

"No, no, Miss Moss! Six bad apples don't make a barrelful!" Mr. Zimmer shook his fist, with the ad still in it, in the air. I decided it was time to leave. I felt for Sunny's hand and took a small step back, ready to make a break for the door.

"Watch out!" barked Miss Moss, and I nearly leaped into the air with fright.

"Watch the plant! It's fragile!" she said, pointing with a bony finger. I turned and saw the horrible plastic palm just behind me. It didn't look as though it could be damaged by anything less than a ten-ton truck.

Mr. Zimmer, ignoring all this, was doing a little dance on the murky carpet. He waved the ad and beamed, looking crazier than ever. "Five plus Elmo equals six," he chortled. The girl at the computer gazed at him, her mouth slightly open.

"Mr. Zimmer . . ." Miss Moss growled again. But he wouldn't be stopped.

"Kids," he crowed, "you've just landed your first job."

We stared at him. "What job?" asked Sunny finally.

"My job!" exclaimed Mr. Zimmer. He rubbed his hands together gleefully. "You're going to work for me!"

○

Mr. Zimmer, it seemed, needed a team to home-deliver the *Pen* around Raven Hill every Thursday. The team he'd had, six sophomore kids, also from Raven Hill High, had gone over to the *Star*. And they'd gone without warning.

"She offered them twice what I paid, to dump me flat," he muttered, frowning all over his round face. "She's crazy."

"Who is?" I asked nervously. I still wasn't too sure about Mr. Zimmer.

"Sheila Star! The owner of the *Star*," Mr. Zimmer exploded. "She wants to buy the *Pen*, and because I won't sell, she's trying to ruin me. But I'll show her!"

"Mmm," murmured Miss Moss. She obviously didn't have much faith in Mr. Zimmer.

He calmed down a bit. "Anyway, don't you worry about that," he said. "Just be here next Thursday morning at five, and . . ."

Maybe he sensed our shock, because he stopped. "A five A.M. start's okay, isn't it?" he demanded.

"Oh . . . oh, yes!" I gulped. I couldn't imagine what Nick

would say about getting up in what he would consider the middle of the night. Let alone Richelle, who I'll bet hadn't seen a sunrise in her entire life.

"Good," said Mr. Zimmer, and suddenly became very efficient. "Miss Moss! Map please!"

Sighing, Miss Moss handed him a map of the area.

"Your routes are marked here. Or you can work out your own, if you like. I don't care, as long as the papers get out," said Mr. Zimmer. "Elmo — you know my son, Elmo?"

We nodded.

"Well, Elmo will join you. You pick up your first loads here. Your pickup points for extra copies are here, here, and here —" He pointed to crosses marked on the map. "Got that?"

"Sure." I glanced anxiously at Sunny. Her face was, as usual, calm.

Mr. Zimmer passed the map to her. "See you Thursday, then," he said. He absentmindedly stuffed our ad into his pocket.

"Um — our ad, Mr. Zimmer," I ventured, pointing.

"Oh!" He went pink, and pulled the paper out again, smoothing out the creases. "Yes. Ah — see to this, Miss Moss!"

"Certainly, sir," she answered sourly, as if to say, you don't fool me with all that "see to this" business. You're not a boss's bootlace.

We put our money on the desk and escaped from the office. Outside, we clutched each other and started to laugh.

"What a place!" giggled Sunny. "Why doesn't he fire that terrible Miss Moss? She's so *rude* to him!"

"Maybe she's blackmailing him or something," I said.

"Anyway, Help-for-Hire's got at least one job. I'll call Tom and tell him. You call Nick and Richelle."

"Oh, no," Sunny objected. "Think I'm crazy?"

So in the end, we decided to wait till the next day and tell them together. About the job. And the five o'clock start. That way Sunny'd be able to hold Nick down so he couldn't strangle me, and with her free hand she could catch Richelle when she fainted.

3

Ruby, Alfie, Elmo, and Pearl

My mother worries a lot. The deal I had with her about Help-for-Hire was that I'd only take jobs in Raven Hill, and that I wouldn't take any jobs without telling her first. That way, she thought, she could screen out any loonies or slave traders who might answer our ad.

When I got home, she was making dinner while my little brother, Pete, sat in the living room watching TV. Monty was watching with him. Monty loves TV.

I found Mom in the kitchen peacefully singing to herself over the chopping board.

"I've found a job for Help-for-Hire," she announced when she saw me.

"What?" I picked up some pieces of carrot from the board and started eating them. Why is it that carrots always taste so much better in little pieces?

"A Miss Plummer down at Golden Pines wants someone to run messages for her, and she wants to pay."

"How did she find out about us?" I asked in surprise, sneaking some more carrots.

"I was talking to the Golden Pines supervisor at the bank today," said Mom smugly, batting my hand away. "I told her about Help-for-Hire, and she told me about Miss Plummer."

"Wow! Thanks, Mom."

Golden Pines was this old people's home at the end of our block, right beside the Glen. How handy. I'd take that job myself.

Then I told Mom about the *Pen*. She approved. She said she'd heard Elmo Zimmer was a very nice man.

"Elmo's the son, Mom," I said patiently, watching her begin chopping the onions with her mouth open. (Mom had read a Home Hints column in a magazine that explained if you kept your mouth open, the onions wouldn't make your eyes water. So she always looked half-witted when she was chopping onions.)

"Yes, I know," said Mom. "The father died early this year. He was an old devil, they say."

This conversation was getting very strange. "Mr. Zimmer isn't dead, Mom," I said. "And Elmo's not a man. He's only in my grade."

She put down the knife and wiped her eyes. Maybe she hadn't kept her mouth open wide enough.

"Elizabeth, I wish you'd pay attention," she sighed, very unfairly I thought. "*Your* Elmo is *my* Elmo's son. And the old man was Elmo, too. Three generations. Three Elmo Zimmers. See?"

I nodded. Maybe.

"Anyway, when do you start?" asked Mom.

"Next Thursday," I said. "The day our ad goes in." I grabbed an apple, bit into it, and made for the door.

"Now you'll be very careful, won't you, Liz?" my mother said.

She was frowning. I could see that the mention of the ad had started her worrying again.

"Mom, don't worry," I said, with my mouth full. "A job with the local paper and one in an old people's home! What could be safer?"

"You never know," Mom muttered darkly.

I laughed at the time. I didn't have any idea, then, just how right she was.

❀

Miss Pearl Plummer was a thin little lady with a very sweet face and a very bad memory.

"This is one of Miss Plummer's hazy days, dear," Mabel the supervisor said. "She gets a little bit confused sometimes."

A little bit confused! That was the understatement of the year. Miss Plummer was nice, but a bit of a headache, until you got used to her.

When we met, she leaned so close to me that I could smell the faint scent of her face powder, and told me that this was her friend Ruby's house. Ruby had invited her to stay for as long as she liked, she said. I saw Mabel making faces at me, so I didn't say anything.

Then Miss Plummer's forehead wrinkled. "Where is Ruby?" she asked Mabel sharply. "There's something I have to do for her. And it's just slipped my mind."

Mabel smiled. "Ruby passed away, Miss Plummer," she said gently. "Last year. You remember."

A shiver ran down my spine.

The old lady stood perfectly still. Her face wrinkled even more. "Oh, yes," she said finally. "Ruby's gone. I'd forgotten." She looked very sad.

"Do you have any little jobs for Liz to do today?" asked Mabel, still in that gentle voice.

"Jobs?" Miss Plummer looked lost.

My heart sank. This was terrible!

"Where's your list, Miss Plummer?" Mabel asked. "Oh, dear. You've put it away safely, have you? Well, let's find it."

So my first job for Miss Plummer was finding the list where she'd written down my first job! Mabel whispered that she was always putting things away in "safe" places. So safe, sometimes, that they were never seen again!

This time we were lucky. The search took only ten minutes. But when we did find the list (carefully tucked away with Miss Plummer's clean nighties), all it said, in funny, spidery writing was: "Liz Free. 1 pkt hairnets (white, fine)."

"Well, there we are!" exclaimed Mabel, as if we'd discovered treasure. "Now Liz can run and get those for you, can't she?"

Miss Plummer looked pleased, and patted her hair. Then she glanced anxiously at me. "You'll be back soon, won't you, dear?" she asked. "I think Ruby has invited Elmo for dinner. And Alfie Bigge. And my hair's a fright!"

I nodded, dumbfounded. Mabel quickly waved to Miss Plummer and ushered me out the door.

"Don't worry, dear," she said comfortably as we went down in the elevator. "Miss Plummer has good days and bad days. Poor darling — she was very ill after her friend Ruby died. And now — well, she lives a lot in the past. But you'll be fine."

I wasn't so sure. The elevator stopped at the ground floor and we stepped out and went to Mabel's office.

"Why does she think this is Ruby's house?" I asked as Mabel opened a drawer and took out some money.

"Because it was," she said simply. "Golden Pines was Ruby Golden's home all her life. Her father built it. The whole street was named for it. The family owned a lot of land in Raven Hill in the old days. Including the Glen, next door, of course. You know they're going to build on it soon? Shame, isn't it?"

I nodded ruefully.

"Miss Golden would have hated it," tutted Mabel. "She loved the Glen. When Miss Plummer read in the *Pen* about it being built on, she was so upset! Still . . ." she sighed. "Everything changes. And no one can have their way forever. Not even Ruby Golden."

She shook her head, smiling. "Mind you, she'd never have agreed with that when she was alive. She was a very grand lady, you know, till the end. And always dressed the part. Marvelous clothes, makeup, jewelery, gallons of violet perfume . . . a real character."

"She must have been very rich," I murmured.

"Very," said Mabel dryly. "And very determined. She had this house turned into a retirement home about ten years ago. She and Pearl went on living here, but it was open to others, too. She wanted Raven Hill people to have a local place to come to if they needed care as they got older."

She handed me some money. "This will pay for the hair-nets," she said. "Just bring back the receipt and the change."

I went to the door. Then my curiosity got the better of me and I turned back. "She talked about 'Elmo,'" I ventured. "Was that Elmo Zimmer? The *old* editor of the *Pen?*"

"Oh, yes," Mabel said. "He was a great friend of Miss Plummer and Miss Golden. There was a little gang of four, actually. Ruby, Pearl, Elmo, and Alfie. They were kids together, and stayed friends all their lives. Alfie was Alfred Bigge — you know the law office up at the end of Golden Road? That was Alfie's. He died over a year ago now, too. But his son carries on the business."

"I work for Elmo Zimmer's son," I said.

Mabel laughed. "Sadly, you won't get many points with Miss Plummer for that," she said. "Miss Golden didn't think much of Elmo's son. Nor of Alfie's. And whatever Miss Golden thought, Miss Plummer thought, too."

I left Golden Pines and walked up to the shops thoughtfully. It was strange to think of those four old people as kids, hanging out in the Glen just like we did. I tried to imagine Sunny and Nick and Tom and Richelle and me sixty or seventy years from now, and failed. I couldn't even start to think how it would feel to be old.

4

Day one

The following Thursday morning at five o'clock sharp, we were waiting outside the *Pen* office door. All of us had made it, even Richelle, who was there in body, at least, if not in mind. She stood in the doorway swaying slightly. Her eyes kept fluttering closed. I hoped Mr. Zimmer wouldn't notice.

Nick hadn't complained about the early start as much as I'd expected. I think he really had thought Help-for-Hire Inc. would be stuck with babysitting and dog walking. Nick wasn't the best with little kids. They made him nervous. They didn't have enough respect, and did disgusting and embarrassing things like wetting their pants and upchucking in public places. I don't think he had anything against dogs, really. But they often did embarrassing things in public, too, and Nick cared a lot about his image.

At two minutes past five, Elmo Zimmer appeared at the corner of the street. Elmo the third, I should say. Mr. Zimmer's son. He grinned shyly as he walked toward us. He did look like his father. Red curly hair, a round face, nice eyes. But his eyes, I thought, were brighter than Mr. Zimmer's. And his chin was

more determined. You get the feeling that he wouldn't let himself
be bullied by someone like Miss Moss, if he was boss of the *Pen*.

"Not this door! Use the back entrance," he called to us,
beckoning.

We nudged Richelle awake, and Elmo led us around the corner to an alley that ran along the back of the *Pen* building. A roller
shutter had been pulled up to show a big, echoing loading dock.

Mr. Zimmer was there, wearing shorts and a T-shirt with
a penguin on the chest. When he saw us, his face broke into a
relieved smile. "Ah, there you are!" he called. "So you *were* around
the front! What were you doing there?"

The others groaned at Sunny and me.

"I bet Dad didn't tell you about the back entrance, did he?"
said Elmo, loudly enough so the others could hear. I shook my
head, smiling gratefully at him. He smiled back. He seemed much
more — sort of — confident here, than he did at school. At school
he was fairly quiet, and never said much. And he always disappeared as soon as classes were over. Never hung around talking
or anything. So he didn't have any real friends. Well, none I'd
ever noticed.

I introduced Nick, Tom, and Richelle to Mr. Zimmer. "Glad
to have you on board," he said, shaking hands with them eagerly.
His eyebrows had disappeared into his hair again. I saw Tom
looking at him with interest. Any minute he'd be dragging out
his pad and doing a sketch. Probably a funny one. Now is not
the time, Tom, I warned him silently.

"Super! The wagons are loaded," said Mr. Zimmer. "Ready?"

Nick pulled the six route maps from his backpack. On
Sunday, Sunny and I had worked out the route each one of us

would take to cover the area. As Sunny had quickly pointed out, studying Mr. Zimmer's map, the way the other team had done, it meant a lot of walking up hills with the wagons full. We could do it more quickly by changing things around a little.

We'd taken the map to Nick's house. Nick had scanned it on his father's laser printer to make six copies. Tom had marked each copy with one of our names, and drawn in that person's route with thick red pen. Richelle had watched, and picked lint off her black jeans, which had gone through the wash with a tissue in the pocket. It was teamwork at its best, we thought. We were quite impressed with the result.

So was Mr. Zimmer. He beamed. "Very efficient," he said to Richelle. "You've planned it all beautifully." She shrugged and smiled serenely back at him. I exchanged glances with Sunny, who rolled her eyes.

We pulled our wagons out into the silent street. It was strange to see it so empty. No people or lines of traffic. Just an occasional car or bus speeding by, a lone jogger pounding along the pavement, and a ginger cat slinking home.

"Good luck," said Mr. Zimmer, as though he was sending us off to war. "Meet back here when you're finished, and I'll give you your pay. Ask Miss Moss to see you into my office." He held up a stern, plump finger. "And remember, a *Pen* to every home in Raven Hill. No exceptions."

We probably should have saluted, but as it was we just nodded and set off, Richelle, Elmo, and I one way; Tom, Nick, and Sunny the other.

The wagons were fairly heavy to pull. Mine had a squeak in one wheel. A sort of regular *gurgle-plop-squeak* that seemed very loud in the quiet street. I felt quite embarrassed by it, as if it was something wrong with me personally. As if my stomach was rumbling or something. Richelle's wagon, I noticed, was running perfectly.

To take my mind off the *gurgle-plop-squeak* I started talking to Elmo.

"Do you always help your dad on the paper?" I asked.

"Since early this year I have," he answered, his eyes on the ground in front of him. "He only started working on it himself then. He's a salesman, really. But he left his job and took over the *Pen* after my grandfather died."

His grandfather. Elmo Zimmer the first. Ruby, Alfie, and Pearl's friend.

"What was your grandfather like?" I asked curiously.

Elmo shrugged. "I thought he was great. A lot of people thought he was weird. He had this big white beard, and he yelled a lot. The *Pen* was his whole life."

He was silent for a moment, then went on. He seemed glad to talk. I got the feeling that he didn't get the chance very often.

"Granddad loved exposing rip-offs and things," he grinned. "He said only a local paper could help local people when they needed it. The paper never made him much money. But he didn't care. He didn't care about anything but news."

"He sounds great," I said sincerely.

Elmo smiled sadly. "He was. Even when he was dying, he was trying to tell us about some big story he had. He could hardly talk, but he was still muttering about it to Dad, wanting him to follow it up."

He glanced at me. "I know the office isn't much to look at," he said, flushing slightly. "Granddad never worried about things like that, and there's no money to fix things up yet." He tightened his lips and lifted his determined chin.

"Early this year, the office got broken into and all sorts of stuff get wrecked," he went on, looking straight ahead. "That's how Granddad died, really. The cops reckon he walked in on the vandals or thieves, or whoever they were. The shock gave him a stroke.

"And it turned out nothing was insured properly. So when Dad took over, he had to borrow a heap to buy all new computers and stuff. That's one of the reasons why we've got money troubles now. That and the *Star*." He trudged on, deep in thought.

Gurgle-plop-squeak went my wagon. I wished it would stop. Also, my arm was aching. And we hadn't even started yet.

"Did you print your granddad's big story?" I asked, to take his mind off his troubles.

Elmo grimaced. "We never found out what it was. No one at the office knew anything abut it. Not even Stephen Spiers. He's the senior reporter at the *Pen*. Not even Mossy." He grinned suddenly. "That's Miss Moss. Granddad always called her Mossy. Dad wouldn't dare."

The grin disappeared and he sighed, biting his lip. "Poor Dad," he mumbled.

I felt uncomfortable, and so sorry for him.

"Sheila Star stole someone else last Friday," he burst out. His mouth was set, and his determined chin stuck out. "Without notice again, too. It's driving Dad crazy."

"Who did she steal this time?"

"Felicity. Miss Moss's assistant."

23

The chewing-girl with the long fingernails. "She wouldn't have been much of a loss," I said disdainfully.

He laughed, in spite of himself. "You're right. She was pretty hopeless. All she had to do was type and answer the phone and take finished pages to the printer and stuff like that. And even that stressed her out."

He shrugged. "As it turned out, we were okay. We got someone better right away. But it could have been a real hassle."

We reached the corner where we were going to split up. Elmo stopped. "We've got to save the *Pen*," he said through gritted teeth. "We've got to."

I saw Richelle turn her head to stare at him curiously. She always thought it was odd when people cared a lot about things. Sometimes I'd try and explain it to her.

"It's like you care about clothes and stuff, Richelle," I'd say. But then she'd just look at me as if I was odd. That wasn't something she just *cared* about. It was life, to her, like breathing in and out. It couldn't be compared to anything else, in her opinion.

Elmo took a breath and looked straight at me. "The *Pen's* been going for sixty years," he said. "And it's done a lot of good things. And whatever Miss Moss, or Terry Bigge, or anyone else says, there's no way Sheila Star's going to take it over and let it die. No way."

5

On the road

I thought about what Elmo had said as I started my rounds, carefully poking folded copies of the *Pen* through the bars of gates, or laying them on front paths. I felt proud to be helping. The work was easy. And I was earning money, too. Then I started to feel guilty. If the paper was so short of cash, maybe Mr. Zimmer couldn't really afford to pay us. Maybe we should be offering to work for nothing.

That was a depressing thought. I tried to put it out of my mind.

After about half an hour, my legs were aching and my right arm felt as if it was about to drop off. I changed hands yet again, and decided that it was quite fair to take money for the job. It wasn't as easy as I'd thought. I plodded on. I was getting a blister. *Gurgle-plop-squeak* went the wagon.

As I pushed the paper through the bars of the next gate, a toddler, with no clothes on except for a bib, staggered out of the open front door.

"Bee!" he squealed. "Bee-bee-bee."

Maybe "bee" was his word for hello. Maybe it was his word

for breakfast, because he headed straight for the paper in the gate, grabbed it, and started chewing it as though he was starving, drooling all over the headlines.

"No, no!" I whispered, trying to pull it out of his gummy little jaws. He opened his mouth, screwed up his eyes, and began to scream very, very loudly.

There were footsteps in the hall of the house. "Jason?" shrieked a voice.

I decided it was time to retreat. I let go of the paper and hobbled off down the street as fast as I could, my wagon *gurgle-plop-squeaking* in double-quick time behind me.

That was my first problem. It wasn't my last. It was getting later in the morning now, and people were waking up. People and animals.

In the next half hour, I was nearly bitten by two dogs and barked at by a Great Dane, which looked as if it could have swallowed me in one gulp. I was yelled at by a man who said I'd pushed the paper too far through the gate rails, so that it bent his rosebush. I was yelled at by another man who said I hadn't pushed the paper through the gate far enough, so it fell back onto the sidewalk.

I was yelled at by a woman who said I'd missed her house last week. I was yelled at by another woman who said the *Pen* was trash and she didn't want it. I stepped on a huge piece of bubble-gum that spread itself all over the sole of my shoe and stuck me to the pavement whenever I put my foot down. I put my hand on a banana slug in the paper slot below someone's letterbox. A little kid came and sat in my wagon and refused to get off. Then his mother shouted at me for letting him do it.

I trudged on and on. By the time I'd refilled my wagon from the bundle of *Pens* waiting at the pickup point, I was hot, limping, hassled, and exhausted. And I felt I was taking much too long.

At last, I turned into my own road, the last on my run. Sweat was pouring down my forehead by now. A couple of boys were walking toward me up the sidewalk. They were pulling wagons too, half-filled with copies of the *Star*. They must be part of the team that had deserted the *Pen*.

I looked straight ahead, trying to ignore them. My face was hot. I knew it must be red all over. My wagon squeaked and rattled. As soon as they were past, one of the boys muttered my name, then they both exploded into snorts of laughter. My face got even hotter.

I reached Golden Pines at the end of the road and stopped, panting, under one of the trees that hung over the sidewalk there. Below Golden Pines there was only the Glen, and the park. So now I could cross the road and start back up.

I looked at the big house set in its huge garden behind the ivy-covered wall. I didn't have to make a delivery here. Golden Pines needed a whole bundle of *Pens* to itself, so Mr. Zimmer brought its order when he was doing his car rounds delivering bundles to the stores and the hospital.

Miss Plummer would be getting ready for breakfast now, in her lovely bedroom overlooking the Glen and the park. She'd be smiling her sweet smile, looking forward to seeing Ruby, to ask her what she wanted to do. Or maybe this was one of her "good" days.

I looked at my watch. I couldn't rest here any longer. I had to get back to the *Pen* office. Cursing my wagon, my blister, and the bubblegum that was still sticking my foot to the pavement, I crossed the street and moved on.

❁

"What are you doing back?" snorted Miss Moss as I peeped cautiously into the office. She put down the copy of the *Pen* she'd been reading.

"I've finished," I said. I edged inside.

She looked at me disbelievingly. "That's impossible. It's not even nine o'clock yet." Then she frowned. "Mr. Zimmer will have something to say if you've missed any houses," she warned. Then she glanced at the paper on the desk. "Mind you, this week it might be a blessing if you have."

I had no idea what she meant, so I didn't say anything,

She sniffed. "You can sit down now, and wait."

I sat down near the door on the long padded bench that ran down one side of the room. I felt like I was waiting for a doctor's appointment.

Miss Moss didn't say anything else. I watched her as she went on reading. She didn't look happy. Every now and then, she'd sigh heavily. The clock on the wall ticked. My feet throbbed in time with it.

After a while Miss Moss pulled a bottle and a rag from her desk and went over to the plastic palm tree I'd nearly stumbled into the week before. She started spraying its already shining green leaves, and polishing them with her rag.

"Would you like me to do that for you?" I asked. Maybe if I was helpful she'd decide to be less unfriendly.

"Certainly not," she snapped. Then she must have decided she'd been rude. Well, ruder than usual. "I prefer to look after this myself. It's mine," she explained. "Mr. Zimmer —" She paused, then raised her chin. "The first Mr. Zimmer, I mean, gave it to me when the plant I had turned up its toes. He said at least this wouldn't die. Or drop leaves." She looked fondly at the nasty thing, and went on polishing its sharp, stiff fronds.

The front door opened and a pretty, dark-haired girl came in. "Good morning, Miss Moss," she said. She glanced at me and smiled. I smiled back. This must be Felicity's replacement.

"Good morning, Tonia," said Miss Moss, barely looking at her.

Tonia went and sat in front of the computer at the other desk, put down her handbag, hung her jacket on the back of her chair, and began sorting out forms and cards. She certainly looked more efficient than Felicity.

I sat on the bench, waiting. The traffic was building up outside on the road, now. And still no one else had turned up.

Suddenly, I had an awful thought. I'd been so busy thinking about my own troubles that I hadn't thought about the others. But the more I did think about them, Nick and Richelle, anyway, the more worried I got. What if the others had just given up? What if they'd just abandoned their wagons and *Pens* and gone home?

Mr. Zimmer will be furious if all the Pens don't get delivered, I thought, working myself into a silent lather. *He'll put something in the paper about how unreliable Help-for-Hire is, and we'll never work again!*

6

Trouble brewing

The clock ticked. Sunny wouldn't just go home, I argued with myself. And neither would Tom. Tom wouldn't stop halfway. He'd finish the job and then complain about it afterward. He was a joker, but he wasn't irresponsible.

Was he? I squirmed. Miss Moss looked at her watch.

And just at that moment, the door opened and Sunny, Tom, and Nick walked in together. I jumped up. I'd never been so happy to see them in my life.

"How'd it go?" called Tom.

"Quiet, please!" snapped Miss Moss. She looked at him severely, and he ducked his head in mock dismay.

"How'd it go?" he breathed, mouthing the words with exaggerated care.

"I'm dead," I whispered. "What about you?"

He rolled his eyes to show the whites and let his tongue hang out the side of his mouth.

Nick groaned.

Sunny giggled. "It wasn't so bad," she said. "Good exercise."

We all groaned.

"Have you seen Richelle?" I asked.

They all shook their heads. "Elmo's around the back," said Tom helpfully.

Five out of six. But where was Richelle? We looked at one another.

"Maybe we'd better go and look for her," said Sunny. "She might have found the walk a bit of a problem."

"A bit of a problem! You don't say?" sniffed Nick. "If you ask me, Richelle's at home in bed right now."

There was a flurry of toots from the road outside. A car had stopped outside the *Pen* door, holding up the traffic. "Thanks a lot!" sang Richelle's voice.

Miss Moss raised her head. We looked at one another again. The car door slammed and the car drove off with a screech of tires. Richelle drifted into the office, cool, sleek, unruffled. Not a limp, or a drop of sweat, or a hair out of place.

"Hi," she smiled happily around.

Miss Moss's grim face relaxed slightly. "Good morning," she said.

Richelle came and sat down with us. "What was all that about?" I whispered. "Where's your wagon?"

"Around the back. Sam dropped it off for me."

"*Sam?*" Who's Sam?"

Richelle opened up her big blue eyes. "Oh, he's a friend of my sister's. He saw me sitting on a bus seat, and picked me up. I had a blister starting, you see?" She showed us a tiny red-rubbed mark on the inside of her foot. "So I couldn't walk anymore, could I?"

"Oh, of course not," drawled Tom. "If you had, you might have ended up with wall-to-wall blisters, like me."

She nodded, unconcerned. "I was quite hot, too," she confided. "And a woman looked at me in a funny way while I was delivering her paper."

"No!" Tom looked around, his eyes popping wide with pretend shock.

"Yes," said Richelle. "So Sam helped me deliver the rest of the papers. He said it would be best not to just leave them there. Then we went to McDonald's for breakfast, because I hadn't had time to have anything to eat, and I was starving. And then he brought me back here."

Nick lay back and closed his eyes. "I don't believe it," he muttered. "And I suppose he's going to do the same next week, is he?"

"Yes," said Richelle. "He said it was fun. And we'll try a new place for breakfast every week." She looked around at us, and smiled. "It's a good idea," she said earnestly. "The car makes the deliveries much quicker."

"Oh, Richelle," wailed Sunny. "How do you *do* it?"

"What?" said Richelle. And the frustrating thing was, she really didn't know.

A few minutes before nine, Mr. Zimmer came out of the inner office. He looked at us lined up on the bench. Tom was sketching, Nick was dozing, Sunny and I were talking, Richelle was filing her nails. He gave us a wobbly smile.

"All done, I gather," he said. "In record time, too. Good work!"

Miss Moss sniffed.

"Anyone called yet, Miss Moss?" Mr. Zimmer asked.

"Not yet," she droned. "But they will," she added ominously. "They will."

As if her words had been some sort of prophecy, the clock hands slid to nine o'clock, and the phone shrilled. Mr. Zimmer jumped. "Come into my office," he gabbled, beckoning to us.

As we went, we could hear Miss Moss coping with the caller. "Yes," she was saying. "We've just become aware . . . most unfortunate . . . printing error . . . yes . . . I'm sorry, madam, but . . ."

Tonia's phone rang and she answered it. "Good morning, *Pen* newspaper," she said. "Oh, yes, sir. Well . . . oh, I am sorry to hear . . ."

Mr. Zimmer put his hands over his eyes and his ears at the same time. "Oh, here we go," he moaned.

He bustled us through the door and into a dark, wood-paneled corridor. At the end of the corridor, we could see a big room filled with desks. That was where the reporters and editors sat, I imagined. But we didn't go down there. Instead, Mr. Zimmer opened another door to the left, and ushered us into a gloomy office lined with books and old wooden filing cabinets.

A huge desk cluttered with papers filled most of the floor space. On the wall behind the desk hung a portrait of a fierce-looking old man with curly hair and a white beard. Elmo Zimmer the first, I thought.

Mr. Zimmer opened a drawer and took out five envelopes. "I'm sorry I kept you," he began. "We've had . . . a few problems this morning. Now —"

The phone rang. He picked it up, listened, and sighed. "Oh,

yes, Miss Moss. No, that's all right. Put her on," he murmured. He squared his shoulders, waiting.

"Yes, Sheila? What can I do for you?" he said into the phone, in a harsh voice I'd never heard him use before. "I know about Stephen Spiers. He just told me. I hope he knows what he's doing, leaving the *Pen* for a rag like the *Star*." He winced, and held the phone away from his ear as the voice at the other end squawked loudly.

I jumped. Stephen Spiers was the *Pen*'s senior reporter, Elmo had said. Losing the delivery kids and that chewing-girl Felicity was one thing. Losing Stephen Spiers was another. No wonder Mr. Zimmer was upset.

"Thank you, Sheila," Mr. Zimmer said, still in that hard voice. "I'm aware of the errors. No. I don't know how they happened. Everything was checked as usual. Perhaps you have a friend at the printers' office, do you?"

He looked up quickly as the door opened, saw Elmo sidle in, and relaxed. He turned his attention back to the phone, which was squawking again. "Sheila. I have no intention of selling the *Pen* to you," he snapped. "I'd rather see it go bankrupt."

"You tell her, Dad," shouted Elmo. He looked angry and confused.

"Good-bye, then," said Mr. Zimmer firmly. He put down the phone.

I felt like cheering.

But Mr. Zimmer leaned his elbows on the desk and put his head in his hands. He didn't look like a man who'd just told off an enemy. Far from it.

34

7

Disaster!

There was a knock at the door. Mr. Zimmer looked up fearfully.

An immensely fat woman in a flowery dress swept in. Her face was streaked with tears and her sharp little nose was running. She was waving the latest *Pen*, open at the society pages. We had to shrink back against the office walls to make room for her.

"Zim!" she cried. "Oh, Zim, how could you do this to me? My pages are a catastrophe! I'll be a laughingstock!"

"Theresa, please!" begged Mr. Zimmer, glancing at us. "Just . . ."

"Every photograph wrongly labeled!" wailed the woman, ignoring him. "Look at this!" She pointed to a picture of a smiling bride and groom.

"'Little Poopsie carried off first prize as cutest pet in show,'" she read. "'Congratulations to proud owner Mr. Ralph Muldoon, eighty years young last week.' And look here! Under old Mr. Muldoon and his poodle you've put 'Glowing happiness for the bride and groom, who are planning a romantic honeymoon in

Hawaii.' Oh, how — how *appalling*! I'll never live this down. Never!" She began to cry again.

Mr. Zimmer looked helpless. Elmo stepped forward. "Mrs. Cakely, the whole paper's a mess," he said quietly. "Names spelled wrong. Sentences left out. Ads upside down. Pictures labeled stupidly. Mistakes everywhere. Someone's done it deliberately. To hurt the *Pen*."

Mrs. Cakely's sobs died down. She blew her nose, and looked reproachfully at Mr. Zimmer. "This is terrible," she announced, as though he wasn't all too obviously aware that it was. "And Stephen Spiers is leaving. After all these years. I can't believe it."

She raised her eyes to the portrait behind the desk. "Nothing like this *ever* happened in your father's day," she said.

Mr. Zimmer sighed.

The phone on his desk rang again. He picked it up and listened. "Yes, Miss Moss," he said finally. "Of course. Give me a minute, then send him in. And please ask Tonia to make coffee." He hung up and turned to Mrs. Cakely.

"You'll have to forgive me, Theresa," he said. "Terry Bigge is here, and I have to see him."

"Terry Bigge?" Mrs. Cakely's eyes sharpened and her curious nose twitched. "Old Alfie Bigge's son? Didn't he lend you the money to get the new computers and so on?" she asked. "What does he want?"

Mr. Zimmer looked away. "We have an appointment," he said.

Mrs. Cakely's nose twitched again. "Isn't he about to build on that land Ruby Golden left him?" she asked casually.

I pricked up my ears. She was talking about the Glen!

36

"I believe so, Theresa," murmured Mr. Zimmer. "Now, if you'll excuse me . . ."

"He'll make a fortune with that, won't he?" persisted Mrs. Cakely. "He's building luxury condominiums, so I hear. Luxury condos next to a park! My goodness, he'll make millions!"

She lowered her voice. "They say, of course, that Ruby was in love with his father, you know," she breathed. "I suppose that's why Terry got the land when she died. Good luck to him."

I exchanged glances with the others. Good luck for Terry Bigge. Bad luck for us.

Mrs. Cakely pursed her lips. "The building's going to cost a lot in the meantime, though." She paused, and finally got to the point. "Terry Bigge's going to need all the cash he can get, isn't he? Even the money he lent to the *Pen*?" She put her head to one side and regarded Mr. Zimmer. Like a bird waiting for a worm.

He smiled briefly and turned away. "If you go out the back, Theresa, Tonia will bring you some coffee. All right?"

Sniffing and wiping her nose, Mrs. Cakely allowed herself to be ushered out of the room by Elmo.

We all moved away from the walls and breathed out. Mr. Zimmer handed us our envelopes. "Thanks for your good work," he said, trying to grin. "See you same time next week, yes?"

"If there *is* a next week," muttered Nick as we filed out of the office. "This place is a rathouse. And even the rats are leaving."

Richelle was looking very put out. "How embarrassing!" she whispered. "Delivering a paper full of stupid mistakes. I hope no one saw me."

I caught sight of Tom's sketch pad. With a few quick, clever strokes of his pencil he'd drawn Mrs. Cakely, waving her arms, while Mr. Zimmer cowered behind his desk. I was feeling awful, and so sorry for Elmo and Mr. Zimmer, but I had to laugh, anyway. It was a very funny drawing. Tom flicked back a page and showed it to me. There was Miss Moss, polishing the leaves of her plastic tree. She looked crazy, and sour as a lemon. Everyone crowded around to look.

The door to the front office snapped open, and Miss Moss herself peered in at us. Tom whipped the pad around so the drawing was facedown against his chest, but he was too late. She'd seen it. We could tell by the way her eyes narrowed.

"Uh-oh," breathed Tom. I elbowed him in the ribs.

Now that the door was open, we could hear noises from the front office. Phones ringing, and angry voices. Some people had obviously decided to deliver their complaints personally. There was a shrill bark. That was probably Ralph Muldoon's poodle, Poopsie, objecting to being called his bride.

"You can go out the back way," said Miss Moss in an icy voice, glancing over her shoulder.

We obediently backed away, only too glad not to have to face her in front of an angry crowd. A tall man in a suit came through from the outer office. This must be Terry Bigge. I frowned as Miss Moss ushered him into Mr. Zimmer's room. How could he destroy the Glen just to make money?

"Zim!" we heard him call as he went in. "How . . . !"

The door shut, cutting off the rest of his words.

"Off you go, now," snapped Miss Moss, glaring at us. She went back into the front office and firmly shut that door, too. We were alone in the dark corridor.

"Psst!" the hiss nearly made us jump out of our skins. With

a creak, a door in the wood-paneled wall opened and Elmo's curly head peeped out. He beckoned. "In here," he breathed. "Quietly."

We crowded into the small, dark space. It was a storage room, full of brooms, mops, and buckets. It was built so cleverly into the wall that none of us had had any idea it was there.

"What . . . ?" began Richelle.

"Listen," hissed Elmo savagely. "Don't talk."

Richelle sighed, and fell silent. Even she wasn't going to argue with Elmo in this mood.

There were voices coming through the wall from Mr. Zimmer's office next door. Elmo put his ear to the paneling to hear more clearly, and Nick immediately did the same. Eavesdropping was second nature to Nick. He was the most curious person I knew, although Mrs. Cakely looked as if she'd come close. I sniffed. I disapproved of this snooping.

But when I heard Elmo's muffled gasp, and felt Nick's arm tense as he pressed his ear even harder against the wall, I changed my mind. I couldn't bear not to be in on the secret. And in a way, I reasoned guiltily, the more we knew about the *Pen*'s problems, the easier it would be to help. I wasted no more time, but pressed my ear to the wall right alongside Nick.

". . . just a bit longer, Terry. A week or two at the most." It was Mr. Zimmer's voice. "Next week's issue has the Molevale Markets sale ads. Twelve pages of them. It's a huge boost for the *Pen*. I got the deal right out from under Sheila Star's nose. Do you know she had the gall to call this morning and offer to buy the *Pen* again?"

"What did you tell her?" asked the voice that must belong to Terry Bigge.

39

"What d'you think?" shouted Mr. Zimmer.

There was a moment's silence. Then his voice continued more softly. We had to strain to hear. "I know you think I'm crazy, Terry. But I can't let her have it. Not even for you. And look, it'll be all right. I can give you half the money as soon as Molevale Markets pay up. And the rest in a month. I promise you."

"What's happening?" whispered Tom, who was crushed back against the other wall, and couldn't hear a thing.

Elmo held up his hand warningly.

"Buddy, I . . ." Terry Bigge sounded uncomfortable. "You know the builders on this condo thing are really pushing me. I'll be in deep trouble if I don't give the go-ahead and pay up soon. You know I'd do anything for you, Zim, but . . ."

"Terry. Please!" Mr. Zimmer's voice broke in. He was pleading now. I shut my eyes. This must be very hard for him.

There was a long pause. I held my breath. I was sure Elmo was doing the same.

"All right," Mr. Bigge's voice suddenly boomed out strongly. "I'll try to stall them a bit longer."

Elmo punched his fists in the air in silent triumph. He beckoned to us in the dimness and we jostled our way out of the storage room. "Let's go!" Elmo hissed. "We've got to talk."

8

Terror in the Glen

We tiptoed down to the big room at the end of the corridor. Along both walls, separated with low partitions, were desks laden with ringing telephones, humming computers, and piles of papers. But no one was working at the computers, no one was reading the papers, and no one was answering the phones.

At the back of the room, around the coffeemaker, stood a group of people drinking from mugs and talking in low voices. Theresa Cakely was one of them. She was whispering behind her hand to the woman next to her, who was nodding sympathetically.

In one corner, a man with gray hair was packing belongings from his desk into a box. That must be Stephen Spiers, the deserter. He shot a look at Elmo, then quickly turned his head away.

Elmo led us out through another door into the place where we'd picked up the papers. The roller shutter that led out to the alley was closed now, and you could see that it had a cute little door in the middle of it through which staff could go in and out during the day. Our footsteps echoed on the cement floor.

Elmo turned to face us. "Sorry about that. But I wanted to make sure I caught you before you left, and I had to hear what was going on. Now, look, you won't ditch this job, will you?" he asked fiercely.

Nick grimaced. "Well, I don't know, Elmo . . ." he began.

"Of course we won't!" Sunny and I shouted together. It was so perfectly timed that we could have planned it. "Of course we won't," I repeated more quietly, looking straight into Nick's eyes, willing him to agree. He shrugged. We'll talk about this later, Liz, his black eyes warned.

"We'll probably have to stay on, anyway," Richelle remarked airily. "If we're going to go on with Help-for-Hire. I mean, we're not going to get any other jobs for a while, are we?"

"Why not?" I demanded.

"Well, because — you know — the phone number," said Richelle, eyeing me in surprise.

We all stared at her. She stared back.

"What do you mean, Richelle?" asked Sunny patiently.

"The number in our ad. There's only one, and it's been printed wrong," said Richelle. "Didn't you know? I saw it when I was at the bus stop. Sam and I rang the number from McDonald's. It's a laundromat. Well, they're not going to take messages for us, are they?"

"What?" exploded Nick. He slapped his forehead with his hand in frustration.

Tom and Sunny looked quizzically at Elmo. His round face turned pink.

"Let's get something to eat and go down to the Glen," I suggested quickly. "You come with us, Elmo."

"I can't go now," said Sunny. "I'm doing a tae kwon do morning class."

"*Sunny!*" I groaned. "Not again!"

"Are you training to be ruler of the universe or something, Sunny?" Tom complained.

But as it turned out he couldn't come, either, because he had to go home to watch his little brothers for a couple of hours. So in the end, we decided to meet at the Glen in the late afternoon instead. Elmo still said he'd come. I was glad. It would be good if he could forget the *Pen*'s troubles for a while.

But when we finally did get to the Glen, far from forgetting the *Pen*'s problems, we talked about nothing else.

The Glen was lovely in the soft afternoon light. Birds were hopping around in the feathery bushes. Chipmunks scuttled around the rocks. Monty lay sleeping beside me. It was so peaceful. You wouldn't believe we were in the middle of the city.

We all felt it, especially Elmo, who hadn't been there for years. And so we started talking about how much we were going to miss the Glen when it was gone. And that meant we started talking about Terry Bigge and his condos. And *that* meant we started talking about the *Pen*.

"If Terry can wait for his money for just a couple of weeks, we'll be okay," said Elmo. "If he can stall the builders . . ."

"I don't see why he needs to build on the Glen at all," I interrupted. "He got it for free, didn't he? Why doesn't he just leave it alone?"

Nick looked at me disdainfully. "Because he's not a senti-mental idiot like you, Liz. He'll make a fortune out of the thing when it's done. You can't expect him to pass that up because of a few trees and possums."

"No," I scratched Monty's ears and frowned. I could see that it was too much to hope for, really. It wasn't the way most adults worked. And Terry Bigge obviously wasn't all bad. He'd lent Mr. Zimmer money when he needed it. And he was trying to hold off taking it back for as long as he could. I sighed.

"Couldn't your dad have gotten the money from a bank?" I asked Elmo.

He shrugged. "He didn't even try. See, Sheila Star tried to buy the *Pen* after Granddad died. Everyone thought Dad would sell. But we talked about it, and we both wanted the paper to stay in the family." His cheeks stained pink again. "I'd like to run it one day myself," he confessed, looking hard at a chipmunk scut-tling up a nearby tree.

Nick raised one eyebrow. You could see he was thinking Elmo was a bit of a nut case, too, wanting to take over a business like the *Pen*.

"Anyway —" Elmo saw his expression, but went on deter-minedly, "Terry wanted to help. He offered the money to tide Dad over. Dad thought he'd be able to pay the money back quite soon. But everything went wrong." He fell silent and sat brood-ing, his chin on his hand.

The light was fading now. The birds were silent. The Glen looked beautiful and mysterious. No one moved. No one wanted to break the spell and go home.

"Next issue will make money, your dad said," I offered, wanting to cheer Elmo up. "That's something, isn't it?"

"I guess so," he answered gloomily. "I just wish we had a good front-page story. We want Molevale Markets to get lots of people into their sale because of their ads. Then they might advertise every week. That'd help a lot. But for people to read the ads, they've got to open the paper in the first place. That means we need an exciting headline. And now with Stephen Spiers gone, that's going to be hard."

Everywhere you turned there seemed to be a problem. I shivered suddenly, and looked around. While Elmo had been talking, the Glen had grown very dim. The trees rustled, and there were scuttles in the shadowy undergrowth. Then out of nowhere an idea popped into my head.

"What about the big story your granddad was on to before he died?" I asked excitedly. "Couldn't you try to find . . . ?"

Elmo shook his head. "No chance. The office was completely cleaned up after the vandals got in, and nothing was found. What's more, Granddad's house was burgled just after he died, and everything was turned upside down there, too. We looked at every single paper before we filed it again." He looked down at his hands.

"No," he murmured. "We'll never know what the big story was now. It died with Granddad. And there's nothing anyone can do about it."

The leaves whispered. I shivered again. And then, without warning, Monty lifted his head and growled, and the hair on the back of his neck bristled under my fingers.

"What is it?" breathed Tom.

"I —" My voice stuck in my throat. Monty's growl became a whimper, and he pressed his head against my knee. I could feel him trembling.

Sunny sprang to her feet. "Who's there?" she demanded.

But there was no answer. There was utter stillness, as if the whole Glen was holding its breath. And then a cool, soft wind sighed through the trees, tumbling the leaves, swirling around us in chilly gusts, bringing with it a heavy, sweet scent of flowers. Monty threw up his head and howled.

And then we saw it. Something tall and pale was glimmering through the trees. It was moving. It was gliding toward us, its long white clothes fluttering. It made no sound. Not a stick cracked beneath its feet. Not a pebble shifted in its path. Not a leaf caught at its long white hair. It stretched out thin arms . . .

Richelle sprang to her feet. Her face was as pale as paper. "No!" she screamed. And then she was running. And we were running, too. Running away from the flickering white figure. Running through bushes and vines that caught at our clothes and feet and hair and tried to hold us back in the darkness. Running out of the Glen, and at last bursting thankfully into the brightly lit street, with its cars and houses and people. And safety.

9

Ghost story

"What was *that?*" gasped Elmo.

I licked my lips, stroking Monty's head, trying to calm him. "It was the ghost," I whispered. "The Glen Ghost."

"Don't be ridiculous, Liz!" snapped Sunny. "There's no such thing as ghosts."

"Well, what was it then?" demanded Tom. "It didn't make any noise. It floated. It was freezing. And —"

"And the dog," shuddered Richelle. "The dog — howled. It sounded awful." She made a disgusted face at Monty.

"Monty was scared," I said defensively.

"He wasn't alone," snapped Nick. His face was scratched and he was frowning furiously. "But it's crazy. Ghosts? I don't believe in ghosts."

"I do. Now," said Tom. He'd pulled out his pad and was sketching furiously. "I've got to get this down while I remember. We're eyewitnesses to a genuine haunting, for goodness' sake. We've got to tell someone."

"How about telling thousands of people?" said Elmo quietly.

We all turned to look at him. His lightly freckled face was still pale, but his eyes were sparkling.

"Well?" he demanded. "We were looking for a big local story, weren't we? So what are we waiting for? We've got to get back to the *Pen* and tell Dad. This is a story everyone will want to read. The Ghost of Raven Hill Glen!"

Mr. Zimmer was a bit worried about Elmo's ghost idea at first. But when he heard what the rest of us had to say, and saw Tom's drawing, he was convinced. Whatever we'd seen, the story was worth telling.

"Now, tell no one," he warned. "This has to be our scoop." His eyes sparkled, just as Elmo's had done. "We'll run rings around the *Star* this time," he said, and rubbed his hands. "This time *everyone* will read the *Pen*. And that means *everyone* will read the Molevale Markets ads. And Ken Molevale will think we're wonderful!"

I was pleased that the Glen Ghost was going to help Mr. Zimmer and the *Pen*. But I have to admit that I also had a sneaking hope that the ghost story might help the Glen, too.

"Maybe the city council will stop the Glen from being ruined now," I explained to the others. "Maybe they'll think it's worth preserving."

Cynical Nick snorted. "They preserve places that are historical, or sacred, or something. They don't preserve places that kids say are haunted," he jeered.

"You never know," I said. I paused. Good heavens, I was

sounding like my mother! Well, that couldn't be helped. I rushed on. "And you know what? I think that's what the ghost wants. I think it was Ruby Golden we saw. I don't think she wants the place where she used to play being destroyed."

"She shouldn't have left the Glen to Terry Bigge, then," said Richelle irritably. "And she should be haunting him now, instead of scaring us half to death."

"Don't talk silly, you two," snapped Sunny. "You know we couldn't really have seen a ghost."

"I think we did," I responded stubbornly. "And when Terry Bigge reads the *Pen* next week, I really hope he thinks so as well!"

For days after that, we were all in and out of the *Pen* office, helping Mr. Zimmer with the ghost story. He was keeping it really quiet. Only a few people in the office knew about it. At his suggestion, Tom redrew the sketch he'd done the evening we saw the ghost. It was very good by the time he finished, even Nick had to admit that, and Mr. Zimmer said that he was going to use it on the front page.

Tom pretended to be cool about this, but I could tell he was really excited. Actually, we all were. Our ad would be running again in this issue, too. For free, of course, since the phone number had been messed up last time. I expected we'd get lots of calls. After all, we'd be quite famous, with our names in the paper and everything.

On Tuesday, when I went to Golden Pines, Miss Plummer seemed to be having one of her "good" days. She had her list ready and waiting. So when I got back from the store with the apples and lemonade she'd wanted, I started to try to find out a bit more about Ruby Golden.

"You and Ruby used to play in the Glen when you were kids, didn't you?" I began.

She smiled and nodded, her faded blue eyes dreamy. "Ah, yes," she murmured. "Ruby and me, and Alfie and Elmo. We had great times."

"Do you think Ruby would have wanted the Glen to be destroyed, Miss Plummer?" I asked carefully. I didn't want to frighten her by talking about the ghost, of course.

She looked shocked. "Oh, no, dear. What could have put that idea into your head? The Glen will never be cleared. Ruby said so. She said it was to stay just as it is, forever."

Her soft forehead creased. She took hold of my hand and held it tightly. "Could you get Ruby for me, dear?" she whispered. "I need to talk to her."

I said nothing. I couldn't bear to upset her by reminding her that Ruby was dead, and Alfie and Elmo, too, or telling her what Alfie's son was going to do with his inheritance. So I changed the subject, and we chatted about other things till it was time for me to leave. I hadn't really gotten anywhere, I thought.

But at the Golden Pines gates, I looked next door at the bushes and trees of the Glen and shivered. And I realized that Miss Plummer's words had at least made me very sure of one thing.

Somehow, Ruby Golden's spirit really was watching over the place she'd loved so much. She knew it was in danger, and she was trying to protect it now in the only way she could. And she was using Help-for-Hire Inc. and her old friend Elmo's news-paper to do so.

○

Thursday morning finally came. We were all at the roller shutter on time — even Richelle, who came in style in her friend Sam's car. They were going to try breakfast at the Black Cat Café this time, she told us blithely. It was a trendy place, but Sam was pay-ing, so that was okay. Great! I was so pleased for her!

With the others, I grabbed at the copies of the *Pen* lying in huge piles on the cement floor, and looked eagerly at the front page. **LOCAL KIDS SEE THE GLEN GHOST!** read the big black head-line. And there was Tom's drawing, looking very spooky and realistic.

"It looks great, Mr. Zimmer," I said. I really meant it, too.

"Glad you're pleased," he laughed. "And look, forget all this Mr. Zimmer stuff. It makes me feel old. You'd better call me Zim like everyone else. Okay?"

We nodded. He looked very happy. And no wonder. Elmo had already told us that they'd checked every line of this issue when it arrived from the printing office. No mistakes this time.

Off we went, wheeling our wagons. I was pleased to find that I'd gotten a good one this time. Nick got the *gurgle-plop-squeak*, and he didn't like it, either. Serves him right, I thought. I still hadn't forgiven him for snickering at my idea about the Glen Ghost.

This morning, I seemed to fly around the streets. The route was easier the second time around.

Hurrying back up Golden Street I met the boys I'd seen before, delivering the *Star*. They'd obviously only just started their round, because their beautiful new wagons were still almost full.

I started to walk past them with my nose in the air. They laughed and sniggered again, but I didn't care. Didn't care, at least, until my eyes fell on the papers lying face up in their wagons. The *Star*'s big black headline read: **THE TRUTH ABOUT THE GLEN GHOST!** And underneath: **KIDS' TALE DOESN'T FOOL THE *STAR*.**

"Boo!" shouted one of the boys, wiggling his fingers at me. "Watch out for the ghosts, Lizzie!"

I almost ran away up the road, my ears and cheeks burning, my mind racing in circles. How on earth had the *Star* found out about our story? What had it written about us? And what was Mr. Zimmer going to say?

10

"How did this happen?"

Mr. Zimmer was *furious*. "How did this happen?" he thundered, throwing the *Star* down on his desk. "The printers only got the artwork for the front page last night. They had no time to tip off the *Star*. That means someone in this office is to blame. And I want to know who. Now!"

Everyone inside the small office fidgeted uncomfortably. The portrait of Elmo Zimmer the first glared down at us.

"Well, *I* didn't say anything, Zim," wailed Mitzi, the editor who'd worked on the story.

Zim's eyes, cold and hard for once, moved on to Miss Moss and Tonia, standing together by the door. Tonia caught her breath. She'd obviously never seen her boss in such a mood before. But Miss Moss lifted her chin and threw back her shoulders.

"Don't be ridiculous," she snapped. Her thin lips straightened into a rigid line. "I frankly don't understand why you are taking this tone with us, Mr. Zimmer," she went on. "The story has been known by six children for an entire week! Surely it's obvious where the leak came from."

"That's not fair!" exploded Elmo. "None of us told a soul.

Did we?" He appealed to us all, and we shook our heads vigorously. I caught sight of Richelle, who was looking highly insulted, and had a pang of doubt. But then I thought better of it. We'd all made sure she understood the importance of keeping quiet about the story. I didn't really think she'd told.

Zim sighed and turned away. His shoulder slumped. "Ah, what does it matter, anyway," he muttered. "It's happened." He opened a drawer and pulled out our pay envelopes. We took them from him silently, and followed Tonia, Mitzi, and Miss Moss out the door. Elmo was the last to leave. He joined us in the corridor, Zim's copy of the *Star* under his arm.

"Out the back," he muttered.

In the large back room, he spread the paper out on a table so we could all see it. I began to read, and as I did I felt my face get hot again. Just about all the things we'd told Zim were there. But because they were put into a different order, with bits of comment in between, they sounded silly.

And what was even worse, the *Star* reporter had gone and told Terry Bigge, as the owner of the Glen, what we'd been saying, and asked him for his opinion. He wasn't nasty, but what he said made us sound even sillier. Like little kids playing the fool.

He said he could quite understand why the local children, who liked to build forts and play hide and seek in the Glen, might make up stories like this to try to keep it from being developed. But business was business, and we'd understand that when we grew up. And all sorts of stuff like that.

We looked at one another in dismay. This made us look stupid. And it made the *Pen* look stupid, too, for reporting what we'd said.

"How embarrassing," said Richelle.

She'd never spoken a truer word. But there was worse to come.

At nine o'clock, the phones started ringing. More complaints. Some of them were about the *Pen* believing some kids' made-up ghost story. But more of them were from people who said they hadn't gotten their copies at all!

Zim called us into his office again. This time he was even angrier.

"You know the rules," he stuttered. "You deliver to every house in Raven Hill! But look here —" He ran a shaking finger down a list written in Miss Moss's spidery writing. "There've been complaints from 21 and 32 Windsor Street; 16, 18, and 24 Sweet Street; 19 Hodgson Avenue; 45, 48, and 51 Shirley Road; 7 and 11 Curnow Lane; 8, 12, 15, 23 Briller Avenue; 122, 157, 119, 67 Golden Road . . ." His voice droned on and on.

We stared, hypnotized, at the list in his hand. Finally, he broke off, tossing the paper to one side. We all tried to speak, but he held up his hand. "I don't want excuses!" he barked. "You just get copies of this list from Miss Moss and you go out and finish the job you've been paid for!"

"Zim — Mr. Zimmer, I delivered papers to all those houses on Briller Avenue," I quavered. "And Golden Road. That's my own street. I didn't miss a single house."

He shook his curly head. "I said no excuses," he snapped.

The phone on his desk rang. He snatched it up, still looking at us. "Molevale?" he said. "Yes, of course. Put him on." There was a slight pause, then: "Ken!" he exclaimed heartily. "How are you this morning? Seen the paper yet? Your ads look great!"

He listened, and as we watched, the fire died out of his eyes and a flush mounted in his cheeks. "Ah," he said. "Well, I'll . . . yes. Yes, Ken. Of course you would be. I'll look into it right away. Right."

He put the receiver down. "That was Ken Molevale of Molevale Markets," he said through tight lips. "He's just had a phone call to tell him that there are bundles of the *Pen* lying dumped in the Glen. He wants to know why he should pay for ads only the chipmunks can read. I want to know why I should pay to have my paper dumped. I could do that myself!"

"Mr. Zimmer," I began.

He turned his head away, but not before I saw his eyes, filled with hurt and despair. "Get out, will you?" he said. "Just get out."

Richelle went home after that. She'd had enough. But Sunny, Nick, Tom, and I stayed with Elmo. We huddled together in the back room, talking.

"None of us would have dumped papers, Elmo," I said to him. "You know that, don't you?"

He nodded. "I know it. But Dad doesn't."

"The point is," said Nick, leaning forward, his thin face intense, "how did the papers get there? And why did all those people call to say they hadn't gotten their copies? Sweet Street was one of mine. I did every house. I'm positive. And Liz thinks she did Golden Road properly, and Briller Avenue, and —"

"And I did Hodgson Avenue," broke in Sunny, wrinkling

her forehead. "And Curnow Lane. And Shirley Road. But I didn't miss any houses."

"Nor did I," added Tom. "It's weird." He began drawing big question marks all over his sketch pad.

I sighed. "I can't bear it," I wailed. "Everything was going so well!"

Elmo rubbed at his chin. "Let's go and get a copy of the list from Miss Moss," he said finally.

We trailed into the front office. Tonia looked up as we passed her and made a sympathetic face at me. But Miss Moss scowled.

"Miss Moss," began Elmo determinedly. "Could we —"

But at that moment, the front door swung open, and a broadly smiling woman in a bright blue suit swept into the room.

"Miss Moss! How are you today?" she cried in a ringing voice. She put down the black briefcase she'd been carrying, and her red lips stretched into an even wider grin.

Miss Moss drew herself up behind her desk. "Very well, thank you," she said tightly.

"Please tell Zim I'm here," smiled the woman. "I have something to show him." Her hard blue eyes darted around the room, taking in every detail, including the neat form of Tonia at the computer, and the group of us clustered beside Miss Moss. Her lip curled.

Reluctantly, Miss Moss picked up the phone and pressed a button. "Miss Star is here, Mr. Zimmer," she announced.

11

The enemy

So this was Sheila Star. The enemy. I stared at her. With her bright blue suit and her jangling gold bracelets, her puffy, waved blonde hair and her red, smiling mouth, she lit up the dim, dreary room like a flare. She looked confident, determined, and slick. My heart sank.

Miss Moss put down the phone. "Mr. Zimmer will see you here," she said coldly.

"That's fine by me!" laughed Sheila Star, glancing at us. "If he wants an audience, he can have it."

Zim walked into the front office with his head held high.

"What do you want, Sheila?" he asked. His voice was steady, but he looked tired and worn. The contrast between him and the bright, confident woman he was facing was very obvious. I felt Tom reaching for his pen.

The woman zipped open her briefcase and pulled out a couple of photographs. She handed them to Zim. We craned our necks to look. She saw us doing it, and her bracelets jangled as she patted her hair smugly.

"Unfortunately, your delivery team seems to have let you

down, Zim," she cooed. "One of our photographers happened to be by the Glen this morning, and took these snapshots. Isn't it awful?" She widened her blue eyes and pretended to look distressed.

Zim handed the photographs back without a word.

"I thought you'd better know," Sheila Star said, putting them carefully back into the briefcase.

"Thank you very much," said Zim grimly. "But you shouldn't have taken the trouble. I was aware of the situation."

"*Were* you?" Sheila Star's eyes widened again. She was the picture of innocence. I felt Nick stir behind me. I knew why. I was thinking the same thing.

"Yes. Ken Molevale called me. I guess it's you I have to thank for telling him about the dumping," Zim was saying.

The woman shrugged. "Well, the poor man had spent all that money," she trilled. "I really felt it was the —"

"The least you could do." Zim finished her sentence for her. "Yes. Well, thank you again, so much, for your trouble."

"I suppose Ken might feel he should refuse to pay for the ads, now," Sheila Star persisted. "What a shame, Zim. I know how you were depending on that money. I'm so sorry."

"I'm sure you are!" exclaimed Mr. Zimmer. He turned away.

But Sheila Star caught his arm and held him back. "Zim, it's time to be sensible," she breathed. "Stop playing around with this paper and all this" — she glanced at us — "all this silly, childish stuff. You know you aren't a newspaper man. Let me buy the *Pen*. Then all your troubles will be over."

Zim spun around to answer. But Elmo got in first.

"All our troubles would be over if you'd just leave us alone!"

he shouted, his voice breaking with fury. "*You* keep bribing our staff to leave! *Your* goons scrawled graffiti all over our building! *You* got some spy to change last week's *Pen* so it was full of stupid mistakes!"

Sheila Star opened her mouth to speak, but Elmo wasn't finished.

"*You* stole our lead story this week and made it look silly," he raged on. "*Your* delivery team followed ours this morning and stole people's *Pens*. And *you* had the copies dumped in the Glen, then got *your* photographer to take pictures. And *you* told Mr. Molevale that Dad had let him down, so he'd refuse to pay. Didn't you? *Didn't you?*"

Sheila Star raised her eyebrows. "Really, darling," she drawled to Zim. "Your son is rather overemotional this morning."

"Good-bye, Sheila," said Zim. He put his arm around the trembling Elmo's shoulders.

The woman smiled, and walked to the door. Then she turned, patting her briefcase. "I'm sure you understand, Zim, that I'll really have to publish this dumping story. It's my public duty, isn't it?"

She sighed while her blue eyes sparkled. "I'm sorry to expose such a respected old paper. I'd love to be able to follow my heart instead."

"You don't have a heart," said Zim.

An angry look flashed across her face. She threw open the door and flounced out, nearly bowling over Terry Bigge, who was trying to come in. She pushed by him without an apology and strode off.

Scowling, Terry walked into the office. "What was that woman doing here?" he asked immediately.

"Coming to crow," said Zim. "And threaten."

"She's a nasty piece of work," growled the other man. He fiddled with his dark blue tie. "Zim, I've just seen the *Pen* —" he looked at us almost guiltily. "A *Star* reporter called last week and said some kids were spreading crazy rumors about my land. So I just said a few things in reply. I wouldn't have said a word if I'd known you were running the story. I'm really sorry."

Zim looked at him gratefully. "It's okay, Terry," he muttered.

"It's not okay. That woman tricked me," Terry retorted.

"She did set up the dumping, Dad," cried Elmo passionately. "I know she did."

"Her delivery team was following us, too," I added. "I saw two of them. I didn't think about it at the time, but their wagons were much fuller than they should have been down the bottom of Golden Road. They must have had *Pens* under their copies of the *Star*. They'd been picking *Pens* up as fast as I delivered them."

"I think you're right," said Zim slowly. "I owe you all an apology." He bit his lip. "I'd be grateful if you'd each run out now and drop off some more copies for the people who've called in. I'll pay you extra for your time."

But none of us would take his money, of course. Even Nick. Sheila Star might have had no heart. But we did.

It was hard to see how much worse things could get for Zim, Elmo, and the *Pen*. But that just goes to show, as Mom says, that you never know. A couple of days later disaster struck again, and in a way none of us could have expected.

It was Tuesday night, and I'd gone to a movie with Sunny. She had a free night from her endless classes, for a change.

We'd gotten off the bus on the main road and were walking home. It was dark, and there weren't many people around. We glanced at the *Pen* office as we always did when we went past, but it was dark and shut tight. Elmo and Mr. Zimmer quite often stayed late at the office. But not tonight, apparently.

We turned the corner and went on our way. But as we passed the alleyway where the *Pen* roller shutter was, I caught a glimpse of something out of the corner of my eye. Something that made me stop dead. A wavering flicker of light.

"Come on!" demanded Sunny impatiently.

"Sshh! There's something weird in the alley," I whispered. The skin on the back of my neck was crawling.

Sunny snorted in exasperation. "You're ridiculous, Liz Free! Can't you see? The little door in the roller shutter's ajar. It's moving in the wind and letting out the light from inside."

I breathed out in relief, because right away I could see she was right. No ghost, then. No restless spirit, guarding the *Pen* office. Just a light. And that meant Elmo and Zim were working late after all.

"Let's go in and say hi to Elmo," I suggested. "We could tell him we've had a great response to the ad already."

Sunny laughed. "If you call three babysitting jobs and two dog-walking jobs a great response."

But when I got to the door and pulled it open, I hesitated. The lights weren't actually on inside the loading dock at all. There was just a sort of gleam, coming from somewhere inside the building.

"Are we going in or not?" hissed Sunny, jostling me from behind.

I stepped through the door and onto the cement floor beyond. Sunny followed. Shadows flickered in the shafts of half-light that came from the back room doorway. We climbed up to it, and peeped in.

12

Help!

The big room where the *Pen* staff worked was completely empty. The only sign of life was a big flashlight that stood all by itself on one of the center tables, casting a beam of light against one wall. That was where the gleam in the loading dock had come from.

"They must be in Zim's office," I whispered. I turned back to Sunny. "Look, I think we should just forget about this and go. We might scare them, creeping up on them like this."

"Scare *them*?" Sunny looked up at me, grinning mischievously. "It's not *them* who's scared, if you ask me. Don't be such a wimp!"

With me trailing behind her, she darted into the corridor that led toward the front office.

"Sunny!" I breathed. But she wouldn't stop, and I had to follow.

Despite the light from the flashlight in the back room, it was dark in the corridor. Zim's office door was shut. Through it we could hear voices. In the dimness, I saw Sunny's teeth flash in a grin. She raised her hand to knock.

And then there was a bang inside the office, as if a box had been overturned, and a strange, rough voice swore. I gripped Sunny's arm. That wasn't Zim's voice. And it certainly wasn't Elmo's.

We began backing away, hardly daring to breathe. Who was it? Was the office being robbed? I was terrified. But that was nothing compared to how I felt when the office door clicked and began to open. Whoever was in there was coming out!

With a rapid twist, Sunny reached across me and pulled open the door to the tiny storage room where we'd hidden with Elmo. In my panic I'd completely forgotten it was there. We whipped inside and Sunny pulled the door shut behind us. I shrank back against the side wall. My heart was beating so hard I thought I was going to choke. The voices were louder now. And we could hear footsteps. There were two men. And they were coming closer.

". . . should be right," one voice said to the other, deep and low. ". . . no use . . . quick as we . . ." The door muffled the words my ears were straining to hear.

". . . might just as well . . . the old devil will . . . lucky . . . back . . . tinderbox . . ."

We heard the footsteps pass us and gradually fade as the intruders moved toward the back of the building.

"Stay where we are," whispered Sunny.

I nodded, though it was too dark for her to see me. I knew she was right. The men could have left. But they could just as easily be still hanging around.

We stood rigidly in our places while the minutes ticked by, not daring to move in case we made a noise. It was stuffy in the storage room now. And hot. I carefully shifted away from the wall a bit. My back was sweating where it had been pressed against the wood. And the wood itself was warm. Very warm.

I thought about that for a long moment. I can hardly believe now that it took me so long to work out what was happening. And when it did, I was so paralyzed with fright that I just stood there for a few seconds, clutching at Sunny's arm and not able to speak.

"What!" she hissed. "What is it?"

I finally found my voice. "Fire!" I gasped. "In Zim's office. We've got to get out!"

She looked at me wildly, then put out her hand to touch the wall. She snatched it back. "Hot!" she muttered. "Quickly!"

We wrestled the heavy door open and burst out into the corridor, careless now of who might hear us. Out there I could smell smoke. See it, too, oozing out in wisps from the crack under Zim's door. Maybe we could put out the fire! Without thinking, I darted up the corridor toward the door and reached for the handle.

"No!" shrieked Sunny, lunging for me. "It will spread the fire! Don't open it!"

Of course. I knew that. I'd heard it in fire safety lectures a million times. But in my panic I'd forgotten. Thank heavens for Sunny. I spun around, not knowing what to do next.

"The front door will be deadlocked," Sunny reasoned, gripping my arm. "We'll have to go out the way we came. Come on!"

We stumbled together toward the back of the office. We'll call the fire department from the back room, I was thinking. Then we'll get out. Then . . .

But Sunny was exclaiming in horror. And in a second, my ideas were tumbling into ruins. The back room was on fire, too.

And the flames were leaping and reaching for the ceiling, licking up the walls. The door to the loading dock, the roller shutter and safety, was completely blocked. Even as we watched, the fire started to roar. Papers on the wall began to catch fire and float around in the air. Smoke billowed out toward us. Sunny slammed the door.

"Back!" she ordered, and again we thundered up the corridor. It was hot and smoky now, and Zim's office door was patched with black as the fire inside raged.

We ran, coughing, into the front office. Sunny closed that door, too, and stuffed a cherry red jacket Tonia had left on the back of her chair into the crack underneath.

"Dial nine-one-one!" she shouted.

So I did, with shaking fingers and a stuttering voice, watching Sunny frantically searching Miss Moss's desk for keys that would open the deadlock that was holding us prisoners.

I hung up. "Soon as we can," the voice at the other end of the phone had said.

But would it be soon enough? I could hear the fire now. It had burned through Zim's door. It was roaring and raging in the corridor. Already Tonia's jacket was turning black. Soon, in a few minutes, the fire would break through to the front office. And we were trapped. My eyes began to sting with smoke, and with terrified tears.

But Sunny wasn't giving up. She grabbed an old metal wastepaper basket and jumped onto the visitor's bench.

"Cover your eyes," she called. And then she was throwing the basket straight and hard through the pretty old-fashioned window above the door, and colored glass was showering down to lie like little jewels on the murky-patterned carpet. She beckoned to me, and bent her shoulders.

"Climb up," she panted. "Get out. Watch the glass. Jump. Keep your knees bent."

"Sunny!" I sobbed. "What about you?"

"I can do it by myself." She glanced back at the door to the corridor. It was starting to blacken. "Hurry," she said through gritted teeth.

13

Escape

I climbed up on Sunny's shoulders, slipping and shaking, and scrambled for the window frame. There were only a few bits of glass left in it, and I plucked them out with my fingers and threw them down to the street. Then Sunny pushed herself upward and I pulled myself, arms straining, muscles feeling as though they were tearing apart, up through the open gap and out into the wonderful, free, fresh air of the night street.

I half fell, half jumped out onto the path. Somewhere I could hear fire engines. They were coming. But the fire was roaring!

"Sunny!" I screamed, staggering to my feet. "Sunny, come on!"

There was a bang against the door, and a scramble, and then a little face appeared in the hole where the window had been. Two dark eyes, a determined chin, a fringe of silky black hair. Then there was a pair of shoulders, and a twisting body. And then Sunny was jumping lightly down beside me, grinning as though this was some ordinary gymnastics lesson and she was the teacher's pet.

Well, I can tell you, I vowed that moment that I'd never

tease Sunny about her gymnastics again. Or tae kwon do. Or anything else. She could take up weightlifting and mountain climbing combined, as far as I was concerned.

We turned to look at the *Pen* building. Smoke was billowing through the empty window frame now, and we could hear roaring and crackling from inside. We backed away, gripping each other's hands, as the scream of the fire engine sirens came closer. All we could do now was wait.

I was shivering, although the night was warm. I thought about Zim and Elmo, at home watching TV or reading or something. They'd heard the fire engines. But they wouldn't know it was their business that was burning. They wouldn't know that terrible sound of alarm was for the *Pen*.

The rest of that night was like a blur. I can't remember a lot of it properly. I remember Mom coming to get me, and her face as she came running up to me and grabbed me in her arms. I remember her talking to Sunny's mother, and putting her hands on Sunny's cheek, then hugging her tight.

I remember the street, wet with water from the firefighters' hoses as we walked to the car. I remember Zim and Elmo arriving and standing watching the whole thing, not saying anything, just staring, their faces pale under the streetlight.

Mom must have taken me home, then, and put me to bed, because the next thing I knew I was waking up in the daylight and thinking I'd had some sort of dream.

Then I noticed how my arms ached, and felt my sore ankle,

and the bump on my head where I'd hurt myself jumping from the window. I saw that it was ten o'clock. Ten o'clock! And then I just lay in bed for a while, while things slowly came back to me.

The whole gang had called while I was asleep, and at lunchtime we met in the Glen. Sunny and I were heroes, of course. Even Richelle roused herself to give us a hug and say how glad she was we were safe.

The others were full of questions — especially Nick, of course. But we really couldn't tell them a lot.

They finally gave up on us and said they'd wait for Elmo, who would be sure to make more sense. But when Elmo did come, he was so silent and sort of hurt-looking, that I think even Nick found it hard to question him. For a while, anyway. But Nick's curiosity always got the better of his sympathy in the end. And so it did this time.

"How bad is it?" he asked.

Elmo hunched his shoulders. "Dad's office is a write-off," he mumbled. "And the back room's completely burned. But because Liz and Sunny raised the alarm so quickly, the rest is pretty good really. Well . . ." he grimaced. "It's black and wet and smells disgusting. But it can be cleaned up. Dad and Tonia and Miss Moss are working on that now. I can't stay long. I'll have to go back and help." He stared at the ground. It was obvious that he didn't want to talk. But Nick persisted.

"Have they found out how the fire started?" he demanded.

Elmo frowned. "Gasoline and rags," he said. "In the back room and in Dad's office. That's why it flared up so fast. And the building's old. Old paneling. Lots of paper lying around. All that."

He fell silent again. Then he looked up. The freckles on his cheeks and nose stood out against his pale skin. "The door in the roller shutter was forced. But the police think someone who knew the building well was involved."

He took a deep, shuddering breath. "I think they think Dad did it," he whispered.

"That's not sensible," protested Richelle. "Why on Earth would someone burn down his own place?"

"Because he's got money troubles," muttered Elmo. "If the building burned down, Dad'd be able to get the insurance money, see, and then . . ." his voice died. His mouth quivered, and he bit at his lip.

Tom and Nick looked away hastily, and Richelle glanced down at her jeans and began brushing at them. They didn't want to see Elmo cry. But I was too astonished to be embarrassed. I grabbed at his arm.

"But that's crazy!" I exclaimed. "Sunny and I know Zim's voice! We would have recognized it." Sunny nodded vigorously.

"The trouble is . . ." Elmo swallowed and went on. "You only heard a few words."

"I'd still know Zim's voice if I heard it," I said stubbornly. I jumped to my feet, and winced at the jab of pain from my sore ankle. "We all know who lit the fire. It was Sheila Star. Or, at least, some men Sheila Star hired. I'm going to call up the police and tell them!"

"Hang on, Free," drawled Nick. "Don't just rush off and start jabbering to the cops and accusing people. They'll just think you're a silly kid being loyal to her boss, or something. We have to get some evidence. Then they'll have to listen to you."

I stared at him. It was irritating, but I could see he was right. I dropped back down on the ground.

"Sheila Star's got a spy in the *Pen* office," said Elmo, clenching his fists. "It's obvious. All the mistakes in the issue before last. And the leaking of the ghost story this week. And now the fire." He pressed his lips together angrily.

Looking at Elmo's angry face, I realized he was right. But who was it?

14

The spy

"Think," Tom urged Sunny and me. He sat cross-legged with his sketch pad on his knee, drawing question marks. "What did you actually hear while you were in the storage room? Maybe there's a clue there."

"I only heard a few words," I said slowly. "One voice saying, 'Should be right . . . no use . . . quick as we . . .' and then the other saying, 'might just as well . . . the old devil will . . . lucky . . . back . . . tinderbox.'"

Tom had been scribbling the words on his pad. Richelle leaned over to look. "That doesn't make any sense," she commented. But Nick's eyes were sparkling.

"Yes, it does!" he exclaimed. "You just have to fill in the gaps. The first man was probably saying Zim's office would burn all right, and that it was no use hanging around and they should get out as quick as they could. And the next one was maybe saying they might just as well do the job properly or the old devil wouldn't pay them, and it was lucky they had enough gasoline to light a fire in the back room as well. And that then the building would burn like a tinderbox."

"That's very clever of you, you know, Nick," commented Richelle.

Nick looked smug. Praise from Richelle was rare indeed.

Tom frowned. "But who's the old devil?" he asked.

"Sheila Star, of course," said Nick impatiently.

Tom shook his head. He flipped back the pages of his pad and considered his sketch of Sheila Star. "No," he said finally. "She's glamorous looking. I don't think they'd call her an old devil."

Nick irritably flicked a stick away from him. He didn't like his theory being interfered with. But I agreed with Tom. The phrase didn't fit Sheila Star. Then the thought struck me. Maybe it did fit somebody else . . .

"Oh, look," said Richelle, looking at Tom's picture. "When did you do that?"

He shrugged. "She came into the office last Thursday."

Richelle nodded distractedly and went on looking at the sketch. I remembered that she hadn't been in the office when Sheila Star came in. She pointed with a long, smooth finger.

"You've got the collar of her shirt wrong," she said critically. "The knot was much looser than that."

"No, it wasn't!" Tom looked cross. He wasn't used to having his works of art criticized.

"Yes, it was," said Richelle calmly. She yawned and stretched. "Anyway . . ." she caught sight of a chip on her nail polish and began inspecting it.

"Richelle —" She didn't look up as I spoke, and I touched her hand.

"Mmm?" she murmured.

"Richelle," I persisted, giving her hand a little shake. "How do you know what her shirt looked like?"

"Oh, Liz, what does it *matter?*" drawled Richelle. But I didn't let go of her hand, and she sighed. "I saw her when I was having breakfast with Sam, didn't I?" she said.

"Are you sure?"

"Of course I am," snapped Richelle. "She came in with Tonia while . . ."

"*What?!*" Elmo and the others sat bolt upright and goggled at her.

"What's up?" Richelle inquired. "You know Sam and I went to the Black Cat Café for breakfast. I told you. We had croissants and hot chocolate. It was very nice. We were in a booth in the back, and Tonia and this woman, whoever she is, came in and had a coffee."

"Richelle!" I squeaked.

She stared at me, wide-eyed. "What's the matter? I've got a right to have breakfast, haven't I?" she demanded.

Elmo jumped to his feet. "Of course you have!" he shouted. His face was red now, instead of white. His eyes sparkled fiercely. Richelle shrank slightly away from him. She probably thought he was crazy.

"Richelle, you're amazing!" exploded Nick. "Don't you understand?" He tapped Tom's sketch. "That's Sheila Star. And Tonia isn't supposed to even *know* her, let alone be talking to her in a coffee shop."

"Oh," said Richelle blankly. "Well, that's strange."

"It sure is," Elmo growled. "And we're going back to the *Pen* office right now. Tonia's got a bit of explaining to do."

❁

But as it happened, Tonia didn't explain anything much. When the cold, angry Zim, backed by Miss Moss, confronted her with Richelle's story, she just raised her eyebrows and half-smiled.

"Oh, all right," she said calmly. "I work for Sheila. Why else do you think she'd have hired a dork like that Felicity girl? Only so you'd need to take me on in her place."

"Get out!" spat Zim.

Tonia picked up her neat, leather handbag, sitting incongruously on the blackened visitors' bench. "It'll be a pleasure," she sneered. "If you think I like spending my time in this hole, you're wrong. Even for double pay and the chance to have some fun with the computers it was a pain. No wonder you can only get kids and an old sourpuss to work for you."

"You . . ." Miss Moss was speechless with rage.

Tonia smiled nastily, and started for the door. On her way, she flicked a finger at Miss Moss's plastic palm tree, which had miraculously escaped total destruction. "Good-bye," she said to it. "You're the liveliest thing I've had to look at for two weeks."

"You can expect a call from the police," Zim shouted after her. "Don't think you're going to get off that lightly. Spying is one thing. Arson is a criminal affair."

Tonia spun around. Now her face was shocked and angry. "What are you *talking* about?" she spat.

"I'm talking about you passing on information about this building so that Sheila's goons could get in and put a torch to it. That's what!" yelled Zim.

Tonia pointed a shaking finger at him. "Don't you dare say things like that!" she shrieked. "You can't pin that fire on Sheila and me. Everyone knows you tried to burn this place down yourself." She glared at him, panting. Then she whipped around again, and disappeared out the door. They heard her feet clicking on the sidewalk as she walked rapidly away.

Miss Moss and Zim looked at each other.

"I'll call the police station now, Mr. Zimmer," said Miss Moss grimly. "Will you meet the police here?"

I opened my mouth to say something, but then closed it again. I didn't have any proof of what I'd been about to say. Only a feeling that there was something wrong here.

Tonia had admitted being a spy for Sheila Star. She had put mistakes into the *Pen* final pages by changing them after hours, before she took them to the printing office. And she had shown Sheila our ghost story. But when I thought about her shocked eyes as she spun around to face Zim just now, I couldn't believe she'd helped with the fire.

But if she hadn't, who had?

15

The end of the line?

I tried to explain how I felt to the others, while we were helping clean up the loading dock. Zim had gotten permission from the fire department to set up a temporary office there.

The police hadn't laid any charges against Zim yet. They had listened to what he said about Tonia, he said, and were concentrating on her for a while. By mid-afternoon, he wasn't thinking about proving his innocence anymore. All he cared about was getting the next day's *Pen* out on time.

"The *Pen*'s never missed an issue, and it's not going to start now," he said, running his hands through his curly hair. "Is it, Elmo?" Elmo shook his head, his eyes as determined as his father's.

"But I don't see how it's possible!" whimpered Mitzi the editor, who'd been called in to help. She looked around at the smoke-blackened loading dock with dismay.

"We have rented computers, and there is a temporary phone line in," Miss Moss told her crisply. She, of course, was well organized already. Her desk was tidy, her rented computer in place.

The plastic palm, only slightly melted, towered behind her like something from a monster movie.

"There should be no real difficulty," she went on. "The printers got most of the pages yesterday afternoon, fortunately. They only need the front section now. And they say they'll work all night if necessary."

Zim bit his lip. "It's good of them. I owe them plenty. But they never said a word about money when I called. Just said they'd do whatever they could to help."

"So they should!" exclaimed Miss Moss. "The *Pen* has been their best customer for more than sixty years! Loyalty must surely count for something."

Zim looked at her gratefully. "It does with me, anyway," he said. You could see he was talking about her, as well as about the printers.

Miss Moss's cheeks colored slightly, and her grim mouth softened, as though she was about to say something. But then she tossed her head and turned away. Displays of emotion were not suitable for the office, in Miss Moss's opinion.

Zim, Mitzi, and some of the others started redoing the front pages. Zim had some story about drains he thought was pretty good. I couldn't get very enthusiastic about it myself, but I guess there's no pleasing everyone. We went back to our clean-up. And I tried to convince the others that my theory about Tonia was right.

"The errors, and the leaking of the ghost story and everything — well, they were just troublemaking for the *Pen*," I said. "Like stealing the staff, and the graffiti. But the fire — that was different. Sheila Star's horrible. But would she go as far as that? And the fire just doesn't sound like something Tonia would get involved with."

"Maybe she just left the door open, not knowing what Sheila Star had planned," said Nick.

The others nodded.

"I don't think . . ." I began.

Richelle tossed her head impatiently, and threw aside her broom. "I don't know why you always want to make things so *complicated*, Liz," she complained. "It's boring. I'm going out to get a drink. Anyone coming?"

Tom hadn't eaten for at least forty minutes, so of course he had to go with Richelle to get something before he fainted. Nick went, too. He said he was hungry, but really he was just sick of working.

"Listen, Elmo," I said when Sunny and I were alone with him. "I've been thinking . . ."

"Oh, be careful, Liz," he interrupted, straight-faced. "You don't want to hurt yourself."

Sunny gave a surprised snort of laughter. I realized that none of us had ever heard Elmo even try to make a joke before.

"No, listen," I persisted. "You know how Sunny and I heard the men say 'old devil will' — well, what if it didn't mean what we thought it meant?"

"What do you mean?" asked Elmo with interest.

"What if what they really said was 'old devil's will'?" I paused dramatically. "What if they were talking about your granddad's will? What if it's got some sort of damaging evidence about them in it? What if his will is hidden somewhere in the *Pen* office, and they wanted to find it, or destroy it?"

Elmo took a breath to answer, but suddenly another thought struck me.

"The vandals that got in, the night your grandfather had his stroke!" I exclaimed. "What if they weren't just making a mess, but actually looking for the will?"

My thoughts were racing now. "That might be why your granddad's house was robbed as well after he died," I went on. "These people, whoever they are, looked for the will in his house, and in this office, and finally, they tried to burn this place down to get rid of it once and for all!"

I looked from Elmo to Sunny, my eyes shining. "Well?" I demanded. "Well, what do you think? It all fits, doesn't it?"

Elmo smiled slightly. "Well, yes. It all fits," he admitted. "But unfortunately, Liz, there's a major problem. Granddad's will wasn't lost."

This only stopped me for a minute. "He might have made a new will," I persisted. "New wills always take the place of old wills. That's the law. The new will might have been the one that was hidden."

But Elmo shook his head. "There was no funny business about Granddad's will. His lawyer had one copy, and another copy was in the safe in his house."

He thought for a moment. "And even if there had been something odd," he added, "why would it matter to anyone else but us?"

"That big story he was talking to your dad about just before he died, maybe," I whispered. "He might have put the details in his will! Or even *with* his will! In the same envelope, or something."

Sunny sighed. "I hate to say it, Liz," she remarked, with her head to one side. "But sometimes I think Richelle is right. You *do* like to make things complicated."

I looked across the room to where Zim, Mitzi, Miss Moss, and a couple of people I hadn't met were slaving away over their hot, rented computers. "I just wanted to help," I mumbled.

"The best way you can do that," said Sunny, putting a bucket and mop into my hands, "is to get moving with the clean-up."

So I went back to work, rubbing at my sore ankle and feeling sorry for myself. Of course, I should have been concentrating on feeling sorry for Zim. But I didn't know what was about to happen, did I?

At about five o'clock, the bomb dropped. The phone rang, and Zim took the call. No one took much notice at first. Then gradually we heard his voice rise. We all looked around to where he was standing at his desk. His cheeks were flushed. His eyes were startled.

"But I can't believe you'd do this, Terry!" he was saying. "Don't you know what happened here last night?" He listened for a long moment. Then suddenly, his mouth dropped and his shoulders slumped. It was as though all the fight had been knocked out of him.

"Yes," he said dully. "Yes, I see." He glanced at his watch. "The banks are closed. I can't do anything now. It's too late. If only you'd called . . ." He listened again. "Yes," he said finally. "I understand, old buddy. No, don't worry. We've given it our best shot. I'll see you in the morning."

He put the receiver down gently and sat quite still for a moment, his eyes vacant.

Elmo ran over to him. "What's happened?" he asked fearfully.

"That was Terry Bigge," murmured Zim. "The builders and the bank are forcing his hand. The fire was the last straw. They know he's got the right to take over the *Pen* if I don't pay him what I owe. They've told him that now I clearly can't pay and if he doesn't take over the paper by nine o'clock tomorrow, they'll ruin him."

"But . . ." Elmo was white.

"He's been arguing with them all day, but they won't budge," Zim droned on. "He's run out of time. And so have we." He put his face in his hands. "I'm sorry, Elmo," he said in a choked voice. "I'm sorry."

16

Surprises

There was a terrible silence in the big, echoing loading dock. Then Miss Moss spoke.

"I never liked that Terry Bigge," she growled. "As Mr. Zimmer always said — the first Mr. Zimmer, I mean — he isn't half the man his father was."

"I don't suppose you think I am, either, Miss Moss." Zim gave a half-smile. "But at least I've tried. And so has he."

He turned to look at his worried staff and tried to speak cheerily. "And, look, if all goes well, we'll pull out of this yet. Terry will own the *Pen*, but I'll go on running it. And one day, I'll get the funds to buy it back. You wait and see."

Elmo fidgeted, and glanced over to us. I had the feeling that we should go. He and his father probably wanted to be on their own.

We muttered our good-byes and left through the roller shutter. My ankle was throbbing and my head ached. But I didn't want to go home. I was furiously angry.

"That Terry Bigge!" I hissed. "All he thinks about is money."

"That's unfair, Liz. He hasn't got any choice," said Tom reasonably.

"Zim shouldn't have borrowed money from him in the first place," Sunny put in. "It's not good to borrow from friends. Zim should have gone to the bank and done the thing properly."

"Oh, well . . ." I sighed. "It's no good wishing after the event."

"I think a bank would still give Zim a loan, you know," said Nick after a moment. "The *Pen*'s had its problems, but it's a good old business."

"But the transfer's got to happen at nine tomorrow!" I exclaimed in frustration. "Zim hasn't got *time* to see a bank manager now, Nick! Oh, if only Terry could get sick and not turn up for the meeting!"

"That's a good idea," said Richelle approvingly. "Let's do that, then."

"What?" I stared at her. She stared back, smiling.

"You're suggesting," I snarled, "that we go and hit Terry Bigge on the head, or spit in his coffee so he gets a disease, or something?"

She rolled her eyes. "You really are ridiculous sometimes, Liz," she sighed. "I'm not saying anything like that. I'm saying we should just go and ask him to *pretend* he's sick."

"He won't do that!" said Sunny scornfully.

"Why not?" asked Richelle. "It's what I always do when I don't want to go somewhere. He probably just hasn't thought about it. But if we ask him to do it — very nicely — he'll probably say yes." She nodded, as though that settled the matter, and turned her attention to brushing a speck of ash from the edge of her skirt hem.

After a moment, she looked up. We were still gaping at her. "Well?" she demanded. "Are we going, or not?"

Terry Bigge's office was up some stairs in a small group of shops at the top end of Golden Road.

We walked as fast as we could, but my ankle really was sore and it wasn't till after five-thirty that we found ourselves staring at the glass door with BIGGE AND BIGGE ATTORNEYS lettered on it in silver. Hanging in the center of the door was a CLOSED sign.

"Rats!" exclaimed Tom.

But Nick coolly reached out and pushed at the glass door. It swung open under his fingers.

"Nick!" I exclaimed. "We can't just . . ."

"We can. This is an emergency!" he whispered.

We tiptoed up the stairs. At the top, there was an elegant apricot-pink reception area, with a shining white desk and two visitors' chairs. A few closed doors were strung out along a short hallway on either side. We hesitated. What should we do now?

The high-pitched laugh from behind the closest door took us by surprise. I clutched Tom's arm instinctively. I felt a bit silly at first, till I saw that he'd grabbed Sunny's. Then there was a rumble of a man's voice. Terry had a client with him!

We looked at one another and with one movement backed away behind the white desk. Suddenly, I think, we'd all started to have second thoughts. Maybe Terry wouldn't be too happy about a bunch of soot-covered kids sneaking up his stairs after hours.

The door opened. We ducked down behind the desk. Tom had to fold his long legs up like one of those collapsible rulers before he could fit. I could feel Sunny beginning to quiver. *Don't giggle, Sunny!* I thought at her sternly. *Don't you dare!*

"Well, darling, I'll see you tomorrow," trilled a familiar woman's voice. "And, Terry, I can't thank you enough!"

My eyes widened. Sheila Star! What was she doing here?

"Your thanks are appreciated, Sheila," laughed Terry Bigge. "But your check will be even more so. Just don't forget to bring it with you."

"Of course I won't!" Sheila Star's high heels jabbed into the carpet right in front of the reception desk. I held my breath. If they saw us . . .

But they were much too interested in each other to look around them. Their feet passed the desk and moved out of sight, toward the exit door.

"I'll let myself out, Terry," Sheila Star said. She sighed happily. "Hasn't it been a long haul?" she said. "But I knew I'd get the *Pen* in the end, if I caused poor little Zim enough trouble."

"You'd never have gotten it without me," Terry Bigge reminded her. "And don't you forget it. He'd never have sold to you, no matter how bad things got. It was just lucky he was fool enough to take that loan when I offered it."

"Poor man," tittered Sheila Star. "He'll explode when he finds out you're selling me his precious paper on the very day he signs it over to you. I feel almost sorry for him."

"Well, don't," snapped Terry Bigge. "He deserves everything he gets. He was an idiot to sign that agreement with me. He could have easily gotten a loan from the bank on much better terms."

"He thinks you're his friend, darling," remarked Sheila Star dryly. "And as trustworthy as he is."

Bigge laughed. "Like I said. He's a fool! Like his father. And mine, for that matter."

We hunched, frozen, under the desk while they said their good-byes. Then we saw Terry's feet pace briskly past us and back into his office. As quietly as mice, we got to our feet and began to move toward the exit.

We could hear the man moving around in his office, packing up to go home. His door hung wide open. It seemed impossible that the five of us could escape unnoticed. But luckily, Terry Bigge was a man who liked luxury, even at the office. The pale carpet was thick, and the heavy door well-oiled and silent. In less than a minute, we were on the street and running (well, in my case, limping as fast as I could!) back to the *Pen*.

17

Elmo's plan

"I can't *believe* this!" Zim's eyes were nearly popping out of his head.

"I can!" snapped Miss Moss. "I never trusted that man. Never! A smart young swindler. That's what Mr. Zimmer used to call him. The first Mr. Zimmer, I mean. If he said to me once, he said a thousand times, 'Alfie's my best friend, Mossy, and I hate to say it,' he used to say, 'but that boy of his is no good.' And now you see?" she nodded fiercely. "He's been proved right."

Zim ran his hands through his hair. "I really believed in Terry," he said simply. "I really thought he was lending me the money because our dads were such good friends. I never thought twice about signing the agreement."

He screwed up his face and punched at his forehead. "Fool!" he muttered savagely. "I've been such a *fool!*"

"Never mind about that now, Mr. Zimmer," ordered Miss Moss. "Now we have to *do* something! We *cannot* let Sheila Star take over this paper." She rounded on us sharply. "Is that agreed?" she barked.

We all jumped like rabbits and nodded.

"But what can we do?" asked Zim helplessly.

"We will simply have to get the money to pay off that — that villain," said Miss Moss, and closed her lips, as though that was her final word on the subject.

"I agree," cried poor Zim. "And how do you suggest we achieve that? By nine o'clock tomorrow morning?"

There was silence. Then Elmo spoke. "I know," he said. He lifted up his chin as we all stared at him in surprise. "Tomorrow morning, instead of giving the *Pen* away for free," he said, "we sell it."

"We can't do that, Elmo," said Zim gently. "The *Pen*'s always been free. No one cares enough about it to want to buy it."

"If they know it's in trouble, they might," insisted Elmo. "If we go around Raven Hill tonight with notices saying the *Pen* needs help because of the vandalism, and the fire —"

"Elmo, please! I know you're trying to help, but this won't work," groaned Zim. "It won't, will it, Miss Moss? You tell him."

Miss Moss frowned and pursed her lips. Then she surprised us all. "I think it's an excellent idea!" she pronounced. "And I think we should start producing the notices your son suggests as soon as possible."

She went and sat down at her computer. "What should I say?" she demanded, looking straight at Elmo.

"Head it, 'Save the *Pen!*'" he said without hesitation. "And then say, 'The *Pen*, Raven Hill's local newspaper for more than sixty years, is threatened with closure . . .'"

Miss Moss typed like lightning. Elmo went on dictating, pacing up and down behind Miss Moss's chair.

When the notice was finished, Miss Moss took it over to the

Rapid-Print shop across the road. She caught it just as it was about to close and bullied the assistant into staying to print out multiple copies.

"They will be ready in one hour," she said when she returned. "I suggest these children call their parents to tell them where they are, and then get something to eat. After that, we can begin delivery."

"Then," said Zim, "I will go back to helping Mitzi produce the *Pen*. If we're going to charge for it, we'd better have a front page, don't you think?"

He went off whistling. I couldn't help thinking that despite everything he was enjoying Miss Moss and Elmo's great plan as much as they were.

I called home quite happily. But my mother wasn't happy at all.

"Absolutely not, Elizabeth!" she said, her voice high and indignant over the phone. "After last night? No way! You come home this instant!"

"Mo-o-m!" I pleaded. But it was useless. The only stay in execution I got was that I was allowed to have a burger with the others, then collect some pamphlets for delivery on our own street, before I came home.

I trudged down Golden Road in the dark, slipping leaflets under doors, still furious and embarrassed. The gang had felt sorry for me for having to go home. Sunny's mother, after all, had laughed and simply asked her daughter if she had a jacket! I felt like such an overprotected dork.

Still, I had to admit I was tired. My knees were shaking with weariness. By the time I finally reached Golden Pines, I'd almost started to be grateful to Mom for being such a worrywart.

I pulled out a whole bundle of pamphlets from my bag and went inside the big old house. The vast hallway, with its lift and winding staircase, was deserted in the yellow lamplight.

Then Mabel came hurrying out of her managerial office. She looked rather distracted, and stared when she saw me. "Oh, Liz!" she exclaimed. "Miss Plummer isn't with you, is she?"

"No," I said confused. "Is something wrong?"

"We've lost Miss Plummer," Mabel said unhappily. "When we went to get her for dinner, she wasn't in her room. Now I find out that no one's seen her since her afternoon nap. Inexcusable! She must be out on the streets somewhere. I've had to call the police."

"Why would she have left?" I asked.

Mabel frowned. "I'm afraid that silly *Pen* story about the Glen Ghost upset her, Liz," she said. "She's been hazy ever since she read it. Talking nonstop about Ruby. And now she's taken off to look for her, I suppose. Dear, oh, dear."

Her phone rang and she whisked off, leaving me alone in the hall feeling guilty. I hadn't thought about Miss Plummer reading the *Pen*. But of course she would. Mabel had told me that on her "good" days she read a lot.

A thought struck me. "She wouldn't have gone into the Glen, would she, Mabel?" I called. But Mabel was busy talking on the phone, and just shook her head and waggled her fingers at me.

I looked at my watch. I had about ten minutes before I was due home, and about twenty minutes before Mom would start to worry. I slipped out of Golden Pines and headed for the Glen.

18

Lost and found

The night was absolutely still. In the Glen, the trees and bushes clustered together thick, dark, and wild on either side of me as I felt my way along the rough, rocky track we always used. I wasn't really scared. *Not really*, I thought. Ahead was the clearing where the gang always sat.

"Miss Plummer?" I called softly.

There was no answer. I tried again. "Miss Plummer! Pearl! Are you there?"

There was a faint, stirring noise. The whisper of a voice. The drifting sound of a breeze running through the leaves. A cold, cold breath of air. Shivering, my heart beating wildly, I strained my eyes to see into the blackness.

"Pearl?" I called again, and stepped into the clearing.

And as my foot hit the ground, a pale figure stood up and held out its thin arms to me. My nose was filled with a faint, sweet, flower scent I remembered. My eyes began to water. My breath ached in my chest.

"I'm here," quavered the figure. "Ruby's gone, but I'm here. I had to come. I had to do something for Ruby. I knew I'd remember what it was, if I came here. And now I do remember. The envelope's quite safe. In the tree that never dies. Elmo is so clever. Everything will be all right now. But just now, I'd like to go home."

Then Miss Pearl Plummer was tottering toward me, and I was running toward her and putting my arms around her small, cold shoulders. And then, together, we were walking out of the Glen.

○

We caused a sensation when we turned up in Golden Pines. Miss Plummer, despite her tiredness and confusion, was pleased by the warm welcome. She smiled very graciously, and murmured greetings and thanks all around.

But Mabel didn't let anyone fuss too much. Within a few minutes, the old lady was wrapped in a blanket and whisked upstairs to a warm bed and a cup of soup.

"And a visit from the doctor," Mabel said when she came down, "though I really think she's fine."

She gave me a quick hug. "I can't thank you enough, dear," she said. "We did look in the Glen, you know. I can't think how we missed seeing her. She does sometimes go down there, looking for Ruby, if she's hazy. We don't say much about it, of course. Don't want to give other people ideas."

She gave me an amused, sideways look. "So now you know the secret of the Glen Ghost," she said dryly. "I couldn't help laughing when I read the *Pen* story. Imagine little Miss Plummer giving six grown teenagers such a fright."

"I —" I bit my lip, and thought better of what I was going to say. Because I couldn't afford a long discussion. I had things to do that couldn't wait, and I was going to have to work hard on Mom and Dad before they'd agree to cooperate.

○

In the end, Mom actually drove me back to the *Pen* office. Since I was obviously intent on self-destruction, she said, she may as well help me — and do some shopping as well. Molevale Markets was open on Wednesday nights, and their sale was still on.

So it wasn't long before I was pushing through the door in the roller shutter and facing the surprised looks of Zim and Miss Moss.

"We're finished, Liz," called Zim. "Mitzi's taken the last pages to the printers. And the others are still out with the leaflets."

"It's not that," I said. I clasped my hands. It had all seemed so clear down at the Glen. But now I wasn't so sure. And besides, Miss Moss was here. I'd really hoped she'd be off delivering pamphlets with the gang.

"What's up?" inquired Zim.

There was a bang from the back door and Nick stepped into the loading dock, followed by Sunny, Elmo, Richelle, and Tom, all looking very pleased with themselves.

"You can't have finished yet," protested Miss Moss. "You can't possibly have delivered hundreds and hundreds of —"

Nick spread out his hands. "You underestimate Help-for-Hire," he grinned. "We have contacts!"

"A lot of kids at the gym took bundles to deliver on their way

97

home," explained Sunny. "The basketball team took some, too. The flower committee at Saint James was meeting in the church hall. They took a bundle each. That skateboard gang took a lot. There was a parent-teacher event at the school. They took bundles. Molevale Markets are giving one to every customer tonight —"

"Are they?" Zim looked surprised and touched.

"Yes. And most important," grinned Tom, "the hot dog man outside the station is, too."

"Why are you here, Liz?" asked Richelle. "I thought your mother wouldn't let you stay?"

Nick looked at me properly for the first time. His nose twitched. "Something's up," he said. "What is it, Liz?"

So everyone was looking at me then, and I had to get over my nervousness and tell. About Miss Plummer, and what she'd said to me in the Glen.

". . . The envelope's quite safe. In the tree that never dies. Elmo is so clever," I finished.

The faces around me were blank. I turned my head and looked at Miss Moss. I could tell that she at least knew exactly what I meant.

"What do you think?" I asked her.

She nodded briskly. "I think it's worth a try," she said. She spun around in her chair and dragged the drooping plastic palm from behind her desk into the middle of the floor. Then she squatted down beside it and began pulling out the brown curly stuff that filled its pot.

"Mossy — Miss Moss — what are you doing?" exclaimed Zim in horror. It was like sacrilege, seeing Miss Moss treating her precious palm that way.

"If this isn't a tree that never dies, what is?" she grunted, tearing out handfuls of brown stuff and throwing it to the floor in a growing pile. The tree's leaves trembled as she worked, and one fell off. But she took no notice.

Then she froze, one hand deep in the pot. A strange expression crossed her face. We all watched, fascinated, as she slowly pulled her hand out. Clutched between two fingers was a fat envelope.

She got up, dusting her hands, and passed the envelope to Zim. He took it, his face alive with curiosity. Then, as we all crowded around, he opened the envelope, pulled out the wad of papers inside, and began to read aloud.

After the first few lines, we were clutching one another in amazement. After the first page, Zim had to sit down.

"Miss Moss," he croaked. "Call the printers. Tell them to stop the presses. If the *Pen*'s going, it's going with a bang, not a whimper. We're going to do a new front page."

"Yes, sir!" cried Miss Moss. And for the first time since I'd known her, she was beaming all over her face.

19

Zim tells a story

Terry Bigge was in bright and early on Thursday morning. He stepped cautiously through the door in the roller shutter and found Zim alone at his desk in the loading dock.

Zim looked up without a smile.

Terry Bigge grimaced. "I've brought the papers for you to sign, Zim," he said, putting his head down and pressing his lips together as though he was very upset. "I'm sorry, buddy. I just don't have any choice."

"You do, you know," said Zim coldly.

"Now, Zim, don't give me a hard time," warned Terry Bigge in a slightly harder voice.

"I've only just begun, my friend." Zim folded his hands and leaned across the desk. "I want to tell you a story," he said.

Terry's eyes narrowed.

"A long time ago," began Zim dreamily, "there were four friends: Elmo Zimmer, Alfie Bigge, Ruby Golden, and Pearl Plummer. As kids they used to play together in the Glen, the patch of forest beside Ruby's house."

"Look," snapped Terry. "I don't know what this is all about, but I haven't got time to sit here fooling around, Zim. I've got a meeting at the bank."

"You can wait for this," said Zim. "It won't take long. When the four friends grew up, they all ended up staying in Raven Hill. Elmo Zimmer started the *Pen*. Alfie Bigge became a local lawyer. Pearl Plummer made hats in a shop up Golden Road. And Ruby Golden — well, she was very rich, and she devoted herself to charity work and having a good time.

"They got older. Ruby fixed up her will with Alfie Bigge, who of course she used as her lawyer. She'd already made Golden Pines into a nursing home and given it and most of her money to her church. Now she only had the Glen to leave.

"She left it to Alfie, her favorite. If he died before her, the Glen would go to his son, in his place. That was you, Terry."

Terry Bigge's mouth was set in a hard line, but his fingers were trembling as he raised them to smooth his glossy hair. "Have you . . . ?" he began. But Zim held up his hand.

"No, I haven't finished yet," he said coldly. "As it happened, Alfie did die first. And the Glen was yours. Or was it?"

"Of course it was, Zimmer!" snarled Terry, all pretense of friendliness dropping away. "The old girl's will was perfectly clear on that."

"Oh, yes," smiled Zim, tapping the desk with steady fingers. "The first will, made ten years ago. But what about the second will, Terry?"

Terry Bigge's face turned an ugly, dark red.

"Ruby Golden went to see you after Alfie died, didn't she,

Terry?" said Zim. "She was a suspicious old bird. She knew Alfie would never have destroyed the Glen. But she wasn't so sure about you anymore." He smiled briefly.

"So she asked you to write her a new will, in which the Glen was left to the people of Raven Hill, on condition that it was kept in its natural woodsy state for everyone to enjoy."

"What a lot of nonsense!" Terry spat. "You're making up a fairy tale to stall me. Well, it won't work, Zimmer! You haven't got a shred of proof for any of this."

"We'll get to that in a minute," said Zim calmly. "I'm nearly finished. You tried to talk Ruby out of making the new will, didn't you? But she insisted. She waited while you had it typed up, and signed it then and there. Then she went home to Golden Pines, leaving the will with you for safekeeping, as she'd always done with your father.

"But she felt uneasy, Terry. You shouldn't have tried to talk her out of the new will. You made a big mistake there. She didn't trust you. So the next day, she made another will, just like the one you'd just done for her. And she wrote a letter saying why. She put the will and the letter in an envelope and hid it away.

"When she knew she was dying, she got the envelope out and gave it to her friend Pearl. She asked her to pass it on to Elmo Zimmer. She knew he would deal with it. She died in peace, believing that she'd taken care of everything. As she always had."

"This is fantasy, Zimmer!" sneered Terry Bigge. "You're just . . ."

Zim raised his voice. "The trouble was, Pearl Plummer was so grieved by her friend's death that she got very ill. In fact, she nearly died, too. When she got better, she'd become very forgetful.

"She didn't remember the envelope she'd put away safely on the night of Ruby's death. All she knew was that there was something that Ruby had wanted her to do. So she fretted, without knowing why. And of course, in the meantime, you'd quietly destroyed the later will, and had produced the old one. The one that left the Glen to you."

"How dare you!" Terry Bigge roared. "You're . . ."

"Be quiet!" snapped Zim. "Just listen. I want you to hear every word! When Pearl read in the *Pen* that the Glen was going to be built on, she called Dad. She was really upset. I remember him telling me about it. But he didn't tell me what came later. He went to see her. He took her out for a walk in the Glen. And there, suddenly, she remembered. She remembered about Ruby, and you, and the new will.

"They found the envelope where she'd hidden it — in a hat-box in her room. And Dad read the will, and the letter that went with it." Zim stared coldly at the other man's white face.

"He'd never thought much of you, Terry," he said. "But that afternoon he found out how bad you really are. Like I did, last night, when I read them, too. And his note besides." He slowly drew the bulky envelope from the drawer of his desk.

Terry Bigge sprang to his feet. "Where did you get that?" he shrieked. He snatched at the envelope, but Zim pulled it away.

"Oh, no," he said coldly. "This is for the police, not for you. You had your chance, Terry. Dad felt he owed your father that, didn't he? He didn't tell you where he got the will, because he didn't want you worrying Pearl, but he said he wouldn't turn you in if you did what Ruby had wanted, and gave the Glen back to the people.

"He said he'd keep the will and Ruby's note here in the *Pen* office in safety for a few days. He said he'd write a note of his own to put with it. Then he sent you off, and later he told Pearl what he'd done, and where he'd hidden the envelope. He told her everything was going to be all right.

"But you couldn't bear to do the right thing, could you? You decided you had to have the money the Glen would bring you. You couldn't give that up. And you thought no one knew about the will except Dad. Without it, it'd only be his word against yours. So that night you brought your goons in here and you wrecked the place looking for it. You couldn't find it. Dad had hidden it too well. But it cost him his life. Because he came back to the office while you were still here, didn't he?"

Terry Bigge stared at him, white-faced. His forehead was gleaming with sweat.

"Did one of your bullies hit him, Terry?" shouted Zim, suddenly losing control. "Is that what brought on the stroke that killed him?"

20

The big story

"No!" Terry shouted. "No! He – he fell. He came in on us suddenly. He started yelling, the silly old fool. Then he just fell. I never touched him!"

"You may as well have killed him with your bare hands." There were tears in Zim's eyes now. "By the time he was found and taken to the hospital, he had no hope. 'Big . . .' he kept muttering to me. 'Big . . . story.'"

Terry groaned.

Zim almost smiled through his tears, and shook his head. "I thought he was being a newspaper man to his last breath. But he wasn't, was he? He was trying to get me to follow up your story, Terry. The Bigge story. The story of a man who'd sell out anyone and anything for money."

"Zim!" Terry Bigge licked his lips. He glanced right and left like a hunted animal.

"Zim, we're talking about millions, here! Millions! I'll – I'll share it with you. We can be partners. You can keep the *Pen*, and have all the money you want to run it. Think about it! Even without your debt to me, you're in deep trouble, thanks to the fire and Sheila Star. I'll be surprised if you'll be able to pay the printers' bills. And they won't support you forever, Zim."

Then he had an inspiration. "Think about Elmo," he urged. "He's a bright boy. He deserves a chance. Do you want him to believe his father's a feeble failure all his life?"

Zim looked at him with something like pity. "Whatever Elmo thinks about me," he said steadily, "at least he knows I'm not a liar, a cheat, and a thief. He knows I wouldn't betray a fine old lady who trusted me. He knows I wouldn't pretend to be a man's friend so I could sell him out. He knows I wouldn't risk burning down a whole street of buildings to destroy evidence against me. He knows I wouldn't leave an old man lying helpless and dying. I'm just glad you haven't got any kids. I'd feel sorry for them." He sighed as he watched the panting man in front of him.

"And it was all for nothing, wasn't it, Terry? Because our story about the Glen Ghost stirred dear old Pearl Plummer's memory all over again. And last night she remembered just enough about what Dad had done with the will to help me find it. And, Terry, I'm not going to destroy it like you would have done. I'm going to hand it straight to the police."

With a growling cry, Terry Bigge lunged at him across the desk, grabbing him around the throat. "You fool!" he hissed through gritted teeth. "You fool, Zimmer. Now I'm going to have to —"

"That's enough!" The deep voice echoed around the loading dock. Then the men in uniforms were jumping down from the blackened back office where they'd been hidden with us. And they were tearing the choking hands from Zim's neck. And then, while Elmo and Miss Moss and all the rest of us rushed to Zim's side, Terry Bigge was handcuffed, screaming, struggling, and swearing, and taken out into the street and into the waiting police car.

The car had only just sped away, and we had barely caught our breath, when Sheila Star stepped brightly through the shutter. She glanced at the policeman standing guard, smiled, catlike, at Zim, then looked around.

"Oh, dear, more trouble?" she cooed to the policeman. "I am sorry. I've come to see the owner of this newspaper, Mr. Terry Bigge. He's a friend of mine. Could you tell me where he is?"

The policeman looked her up and down. "Mr. Bigge's on his way to jail," he said stolidly. "He's under arrest." He took out a little black book. "Perhaps you'd like to leave your name?" he suggested.

Sheila Star's smile disappeared. Her jaw dropped. "Oh!" she squeaked, and backed away. "Oh, no, that won't be necessary!" She spun around and almost ran out the door, stumbling slightly as she went.

Tom made a rude noise. Miss Moss laughed maliciously. And even Zim managed a smile.

Sheila Star wouldn't feel like coming back to the *Pen* for a long, long time.

By the time the printers' trucks arrived and unloaded the new *Pens* half an hour later, things seemed more normal. A policeman was still on guard outside, but Zim was sitting at his desk and drinking a cup of coffee.

After the trucks had gone, we pulled down the roller shutter and held up the paper to show him. **GOLDEN PINES WILL SEN-SATION!** proclaimed the headline in thick black type. And underneath: **HEIRESS LEAVES GLEN TO PEOPLE.**

"Looks great, Dad," enthused Elmo.

Miss Moss, hovering around the back of Zim's chair, nodded vigorously. "It certainly does," she said. "It's a great issue."

Zim smiled ruefully, and stroked his tender throat. "Well, I'm glad," he said. "Since it'll probably be our last."

We fell silent, and he looked down into his cup, swirling the liquid around and around. "Got to face facts," he said. "Terry Bigge was right about one thing, at least. The printers can't go on carrying us. We're finished."

"You're forgetting about people paying for the paper this issue, Dad," Elmo objected.

Zim squeezed his arm. "Look, Elmo, and all of you," he said. "You know how much I appreciate all you've done. But I don't know that there's as much good feeling toward the *Pen* as you think. Especially lately. Dad was a great editor. But I . . ." His voice trailed off. He pressed his lips together.

"Anyway," he went on more briskly, "it's past nine. We're very late getting the paper out. So —"

The door in the roller shutter creaked open. Noise from the street beat in on us. "Excuse me, sir," called the policeman. "Ah — could you come here a moment?"

Zim heaved himself to his feet and walked over to him. We followed.

"What's gone wrong *now?*" muttered Nick.

21

Help for hire!

The policeman was jerking his head out through the door and into the street. "The lieutenant around the corner at the front entrance has been having a bit of trouble," he muttered, rubbing at his mouth to hide a smile. "Seems a few people want to buy a paper. He sent them around here. They say the delivery's late and they can't wait, so they've come here to buy in person."

Zim's eyebrows shot up in surprise. "Really?" he exclaimed. He popped his head out the door. There was a roaring noise. The policeman's grin broadened. Zim jerked back and spun around to us. His eyes were wide. His mouth was open. He couldn't speak. Just pointed.

So then we looked, too, and saw what he had seen. A chattering line of people that stretched up the street and around the corner. A cheering, chanting crowd waving money in the air. "Save the *Pen*!" they were calling. "Save the *Pen*!"

"Miss Moss!" squeaked Zim, clutching at his hair, and beginning to tear at the bundles of newspapers with his bare hands. "Get the petty cash box!"

But we didn't really need the petty cash box. No one wanted

change. They just wanted to donate some money to help. We worked frantically, but the more *Pens* we sold, the more people arrived to join the line, which soon snaked right around the corner and created chaos.

By lunchtime, the *Pens* were all gone. We put up notices to say so. We ran along the line, telling everyone. But then people started just coming in and handing over their donations without expecting anything in return. And almost every one of them had a word of praise for the paper, or a handshake for Zim, who simply stood, amazed, as the pile of cash grew.

When a nurse from Golden Pines came with a plastic bag full of coins from the residents, he was surprised. When Ralph Muldoon grandly jumped the line with Poopsie under his arm to hand over a hundred dollars, mumbling that "mistakes will happen" and "sorry to hear about the problems, my boy," he was astounded. When the manager of Molevale Markets came in with a check, he was flabbergasted.

"When you kids spread the word, you certainly spread the word," he muttered to us.

Nick puffed out his chest. "We're not called Help-for-Hire for nothing," he said.

So that's how the *Raven Hill Pen*, and the Glen, were saved. At the police station, Terry Bigge finally admitted everything and named the man who had helped him burn the office.

He tried to pull Sheila Star down with him, too, but no one really believed she'd had anything to do with the will or the fire.

She was just a mischief-maker who thought she was using Terry to get something she wanted. But all the time he was really using her, of course, to help him destroy the *Pen* and make sure old Mr. Zimmer's evidence against him was never found. She got off with a warning. Terry Bigge was sent to jail.

Zim made enough money that famous Thursday to give the printers everything he owed them. The insurance people paid up, and the *Pen* office was fixed and redecorated so that it was much, much nicer and brighter than it had been before. Miss Moss was nicer and brighter, too. She kept her plastic palm tree, though. She said it had even more sentimental value for her now.

I went on going to see Miss Plummer every week. But I never talked to her, or anyone, about the night I found her in the Glen.

I never talked to her about how odd it was that when the Golden Pines staff looked for her there, they couldn't see her. Almost as though someone was hiding her from them. I never talked about the soft wind that had stirred the leaves where there had been utter stillness a moment before. Or the chill breath that made me shiver. And I never mentioned the traces of sweet flower perfume that had filled the clearing. I thought I'd better not. Miss Plummer didn't wear strong perfume. But Ruby always did. She loved the scent of violets.

What I figured was, Ruby Golden had done what she wanted to do, and now she could be at peace. There was no need to start the whole thing up again. Besides, I had about as much on my plate as I could handle. We'd all had our pictures in the paper, you see. And so Help-for-Hire Inc. was launched in a blaze of publicity that opened even Richelle's eyes. For a minute.

I think the thing we were most proud of was our teamwork.

Because when you came to think about it, the different talents of all of us had played a part in solving the *Pen* mystery. And strangely enough it was the talents we *didn't* mention in our ad that were most important.

Tom's drawing of Sheila Star helped unmask Tonia, the spy. Sunny's gymnastics saved her and me from the fire. Nick's cool curiosity got us into Terry Bigge's office. My bleeding heart, as Nick insultingly put it, made me make friends with Miss Plummer, and go to look for her when she was missing.

And Richelle? Even her eye for clothes came in. Because I don't think she'd have even mentioned seeing Tonia at the Black Cat Café, if Tom's sketch hadn't gotten Sheila Star's blouse a bit wrong.

We asked Elmo to join us. He adds determination to the mix. I've never met such a determined boy. So there are six Help-for-Hire kids now. Just as well, too. We've been inundated with work since the story in the paper.

And it's not all babysitting and dog walking, either. Some of the things we've been asked to do would curl your hair! Even Nick says it's interesting. Mind you, as he says, it's hard to see how *anything* could outdo our first job.

But, as my mom says, you never know.

Help-for-Hire cracked their first case! Will they survive their next? Find out what happens when Tom faces off against a dangerous criminal known only as the Gripper.

Here's a sneak peak from:

EMILY RODDA'S
RAVEN HILL MYSTERIES

#2: THE SORCERER'S APPRENTICE

The name Jack the Gripper started as a joke, but there was nothing funny about what the thief himself was up to. He was vicious, always attacking from behind, whipping his arm around his victims' necks, and pulling it so tight they couldn't breathe. There was also something poking the victim in the back—possibly the hard point of a gun barrel.

Then he'd grab their bag or wallet and whisper, "Now I'm going to let you live and you're going to shut up. Got it? Keep your eyes closed till you count to fifty!"

It was always the same method and the same words. By the time a victim finished counting, the Gripper was gone. And the strange thing was, nobody ever saw a man running from the scene of the crime. Nobody ever saw anything suspicious at all. It was like the Gripper disappeared into thin air.

He usually went for his victims after dark, but occasionally an old man or woman alone in a parking lot in broad daylight would be too much of a temptation for him. So he'd rip them off as quick as a flash — and still get clean away.

I heard this lady on a call-in radio show saying that she thought he had supernatural powers. That's what she thought, anyway. Of course I don't believe in things like that. But even with cops crawling all over Raven Hill, the attacks continued and nobody ever saw a thing. The Gripper was smart, no doubt about that.

At first, there were robberies once or twice a week, but soon they were happening almost every day. The Gripper hadn't killed anyone yet, but the police were obviously worried that he might. The attacks were getting more violent. More and more victims ended up on the ground, gasping for breath, and had to be taken to the hospital for observation.

Of course there were a lot of sick jokes going around at Raven Hill High. But we weren't kidding ourselves. Everybody was walking around town looking over their shoulders for Jack the Gripper — even us kids.

Anyway, let me tell you how Help-for-Hire Inc. got involved in all this. . . .

THEIR NEXT TRICK...
MAKE CRIME DISSAPEAR

EMILY RODDA'S
RAVEN HILL MYSTERIES

#2: THE SORCERER'S APPRENTICE

■SCHOLASTIC

Given a chance to help out at a local magic shop, the kids are thrilled—until a shocking crime spree means it won't be all fun and games.

Welcome to Raven Hill. . .where danger means business.

■ SCHOLASTIC

RH2T

EMILY RODDA'S
DELTORA

___ 0-439-25323-3	**Deltora Quest #1: The Forest of Silence**	$4.99 US
___ 0-439-25324-1	**Deltora Quest #2: The Lake of Tears**	$4.99 US
___ 0-439-25325-X	**Deltora Quest #3: City of the Rats**	$4.99 US
___ 0-439-25326-8	**Deltora Quest #4: The Shifting Sands**	$4.99 US
___ 0-439-25327-6	**Deltora Quest #5: Dread Mountain**	$4.99 US
___ 0-439-25328-4	**Deltora Quest #6: The Maze of the Beast**	$4.99 US
___ 0-439-25329-2	**Deltora Quest #7: The Valley of the Lost**	$4.99 US
___ 0-439-25330-6	**Deltora Quest #8: Return to Del**	$4.99 US
___ 0-439-39491-0	**Deltora Shadowlands #1: Cavern of the Fear**	$4.99 US
___ 0-439-39492-9	**Deltora Shadowlands #2: The Isle of Illusion**	$4.99 US
___ 0-439-39493-7	**Deltora Shadowlands #3: The Shadowlands**	$4.99 US
___ 0-439-63373-7	**Dragons of Deltora #1: Dragon's Nest**	$4.99 US
___ 0-439-63374-5	**Dragons of Deltora #2: Shadowgate**	$4.99 US
___ 0-439-63375-3	**Dragons of Deltora #3: Isle of the Dead**	$4.99 US
___ 0-439-63376-1	**Dragons of Deltora #4: Sisters of the South**	$4.99 US
___ 0-439-73647-1	**How to Draw Deltora Monsters**	$5.99 US
___ 0-439-39084-2	**Deltora Book of Monsters**	$7.99 US

Available wherever you buy books, or use this order form.

Scholastic Inc., P.O. Box 7502, Jefferson City, MO 65102

Please send me the books I have checked above. I am enclosing $_____ (please add $2.00 to cover shipping and handling). Send check or money order—no cash or C.O.D.s please.

Name_____Age_____

Address_____

City_____State/Zip_____

Please allow four to six weeks for delivery. Offer good in the U.S. only. Sorry, mail orders are not available to residents of Canada. Prices subject to change.

Go to www.scholastic.com/deltora to learn more about the mysterious land

SCHOLASTIC